As Good As Dead

A Douglas Files Short

Nathan Birr

Published by BEACON BOOKS, LLC

Image used under license from Shutterstock.com

ISBN: 978-1-7321373-7-0 (sc)

www.nathanbirr.com

Also by Nathan Birr

The Douglas Files:
Overnight Delivery – Book One
Three's a Crowd – Book Two
All an Illusion – Book Three
Shot List – Book Four
Chasing the Wind – Book Five
Blood and Treasure – Book Six
One Life to Lose – Book Seven
Golden Key – Book Eight
Mine to Avenge – Book Nine

Black Male – Short
WinterKill – Short
Short Sail - Short

Last Resort Series
Fire & Ice
Broken Trust

God, Girls, Golf & the Gridiron
(Not Always in That Order) . . . A Love Story

All is Calm?

The Book of Levi

Augusta Whispers

To the ones who would come looking for me . . .

Chapter One

Friday, October 18, 2013
7:29 a.m.

DETECTIVE ASHLEY LARSON twirled a finger through her shoulder-length blond hair and sighed at traffic on Santa Monica Boulevard. This was one part of L.A. she didn't miss. In fact, after four and a half months, she was finding there weren't many parts she did miss. This her first visit back, she'd expected waves of nostalgia and sadness to wash over her upon seeing familiar landmarks and her old haunts. Hadn't been the case. It was a little weird, being here as a visitor, but she had no regrets.

She smiled to herself as the light changed and she accelerated. No regrets. She was two weeks and a day from marrying a man she'd never dated, her former partner of three years, who had proposed out of the blue. Plenty of people—including her dad—had told her it was crazy, getting married to your best friend, getting married so soon—just six months after his proposal. But she'd never regretted her decision to say yes, to uproot her life and career, to move to Northern California and make a life with Dylan. Never regretted it, and in fact was growing more and more sure of her decision by the day.

A box truck pulled from the curb in front of her, and she quit reminiscing and concentrated on traffic. She had grown used to whipping in and out of Redding's nominal traffic in her Beetle convertible, not navigating L.A.'s hustle and flow in this boxy SUV—a Nissan Rogue—she'd rented at the airport the day before. She wondered what traffic in Mexico would be like. She'd never been, never had an interest in crossing the border—unless it was to an all-inclusive in Puerto Vallarta or Cabo. But not on a detective's salary.

Mexico.

The absurdity of it hit her as she hit the brakes for another stoplight. Hers and Dylan's was going to be a simple wedding, and yet, two weeks out, she should be the busy bride-to-be, scurrying around making final arrangements and tying up loose ends. That or planning for and dreaming of the future. Instead, she was giving up her penultimate weekend as a single woman to chase to Mexico on what was, in all likelihood, a failed mission.

And one she still wasn't one hundred percent certain why she had instigated.

*   *   *

Nine days ago . . .
Wednesday, October 9
5:09 p.m.

ASHLEY STEPPED out into the searing heat, intensified as it beat down on the blacktop of the Redding Police Department parking lot. The ping of an aluminum bat connecting with a softball and ensuing cheers wafted on the breeze from a nearby ballfield. That breeze did little to cool the oven-like air. Moving north, Ashley had expected temperatures to cool down, but Redding was setting all sorts of heat records. So she turned her attention from the sweat quickly beading on her brow to her phone. It had vibrated with a call while she was finishing up a case report, and she hadn't bothered to check it until now.

The number was familiar, one with which she had been playing phone tag most of the day. No voicemail. As she beeped her car open, she tapped redial. The phone purred in her ear as she entered a sauna, quickly starting the car and lowering the windows while also cranking the A/C. Three rings, then, "This is Sam."

"Sam, it's Ashley Larson. Sorry I missed you."

"It's no problem," came the high, soft reply. "You said in your initial voicemail you had questions about Jackson?"

"Yeah," Ashley answered as she backed out of her parking stall. "Short of it is, I've been trying to get ahold of him for several weeks and he's not answering his phone. It's like he's ghosting me. I called Reggie, and we swapped voicemails for most of Monday, and all I got out of him was that Jackson had gone to Mexico for a while. He's in Nebraska now—Reggie, I mean—visiting his mother or his grandmother or something, so I'm trying the rest of Jackson's friends, hoping some of them know more than 'he's in Mexico.'"

Sam was silent for a moment, maybe processing.

"Sorry, that was a mouthful," Ashley said.

"No, it's fine," Sam said. "Thing is, I've been trying to get ahold of him for a while too. No luck."

"Are you and he . . . dating?"

"No."

"I ask because I didn't want you to think I was stepping on your territory."

"You're not."

"I'm getting married in less than a month," Ashley said, pausing to swipe down her sun visor.

"Congratulations."

"Thanks. I invited Jackson but he never RSVP'd, and maybe I'm just going bridezilla here, but he's an important part of my life and Dylan's life, and I want him to be there. More than that, I want to know what's going on." She sighed. "But if you don't know any more . . . Didn't we play this game a few months ago?"

Sam was quiet again.

"When was the last time you talked to him?" Ashley asked.

"We talked after the thing with the Russians, so back in April sometime."

"And that's the last you've heard from him?"

"Not exactly."

Ashley coasted to a yield, then gunned the engine to beat traffic north on Market Street. "What do you mean 'not exactly'?"

"Like you said, I've tried to get ahold of him a few times, and he hasn't answered or returned my calls. I even stopped by his house, and he wasn't there."

"This is like the last time," Ashley said.

"So I went to Reggie, about a week and a half ago, actually. He told me Jackson had gone down to Mexico in early September. To Tijuana."

Ashley frowned. "What the heck is he doing in Tijuana? Working a case?"

"That's what I asked Reggie. His answer was 'getting away.'"

"Getting away?"

"His exact words," Sam said.

"He say anything else?"

"Said he'd been there for most of the month."

"Of September?"

"Yes."

"Doing what?" Ashley asked as she turned into the Safeway parking lot. It was her night to make dinner, and she'd decided she was too hot to cook and so she and Dylan would have to settle for salads. To wit, she needed some greens.

"Reggie didn't know," Sam answered. "He said life had taken its toll and Jackson needed to get away."

"And he chose Mexico? He hates Mexico."

"I said something similar to Reggie, and he just shrugged."

"Being coy or does he not know anything more?"

"My take was he didn't know, that Jackson hadn't looped him in."

"He say that?"

"Not in so many words. More of how he said it."

Ashley digested as she searched for a parking spot. Close, if preferable, lest she melt on the walk in. "Has Reggie been in touch with him at all?"

Sam hesitated for a second. "He said he got a postcard a few days after Jackson left."

"A postcard?"

"A picture of the surf on the beach, Tijauna scrawled in bright letters on the front. He showed it to me."

"What'd it say?"

"'*Reg, the women here are indeed muy caliente!*' with an exclamation point. Signed '*Jack.*'"

4

"The women here are *muy caliente?*"

"Yeah," Sam said softly.

"So Jackson is so bummed with life that he went down to troll for *señoritas* in Tijuana?"

"That's what it sounded like."

Ashley finally found a spot and veered into it, stopping on a dime. "And that settled okay with you?"

"No, but I didn't know what to do about it. Now . . . I'm still not sure."

Ashley hesitated, trying to figure out if there was jealousy in Sam's words or not. The downside of a phone conversation—you couldn't look somebody in the eyes to see what they were feeling. She let it pass.

"Neither am I," Ashley said. "I'm out of people to call."

"Did you try Jackson's grandpa?"

"Leroy?"

"Yeah."

"No. I'll try that. Thanks, Sam. I'll let you know if I hear any update."

"Me too."

Ashley ended the call and sat back for a second, trying to place the emotions she'd heard in Sam's voice. She concluded that only one was prominent—anxiety.

*   *   *

Friday, October 18
7:41 a.m.

AS THEY turned onto Colorado Avenue and passed under the Santa Monica arch, it became real for Samantha MacRaney. She was going to Mexico.

It had been real when she'd packed the night before, when she'd rearranged shifts at the hospital where she worked as a nurse, when she'd called Steve to let him know—sort of—what she was doing. She'd been expecting anything between a reprimand and a direct command from her older brother, but he'd seemed preoccupied with *his* news—he had a girlfriend, and apparently it was serious. Where had that come from?

Hers was apparently not the only life moving fast.

They coasted down the ramp and onto the wooden Santa Monica Pier. It brought back a tinge of sadness to Sam. Her first "date" with Jeff had been here. A visit to the aquarium, fresh seafood for dinner, ice cream at sunset. It had been a romance to match the summer, coming out of the blue, moving fast, and ending before she knew it.

Jeff wasn't the only guy brought to mind by the pier. Sam and Jackson had gone there several times on "dates." They'd never had a formal relationship, but Sam didn't know what else to call it but dating. What with her relationship with Jeff, dealing with her mom's breast cancer diagnosis (she was currently three-months cancer free!), and the usual hectic schedule of an E.R. nurse, Sam had all but forgotten about Jackson, about what they'd had—even if neither of them had been able to define it. Now he, and thus it, was back on the forefront of her brain.

Ashley turned so suddenly that Sam had to brace herself against the door.

"Sorry," the diminutive detective said. She had flown down the night before, and Sam had let her crash at her apartment instead of getting a hotel. It also saved Sam a drive to the pier and parking fees.

"It's okay," Sam said.

"Jackson used to have conniptions about my driving."

The pier provided twenty-four-hour parking, and served as a reasonable meeting location. Even though she was driving to Mexico, Ashley took a ticket for the lot, which at twenty to eight was mostly empty. So was the pier, and the beach. That had as much to do with overcast, breezy skies as the early hour, Sam figured.

Ashley parked, and they both got out. The ocean was gray and angry, crashing onshore in thunderous waves. Sam quickly put her hair in a ponytail to keep it out of her face and scanned the pier. Her eyes wandered to the beach, and with them her mind, back to a year and a half ago when she and Jackson had celebrated his birthday by coming to the pier for ice cream cones and a walk along the shoreline. She remembered the talk they'd had that night, about him trying to cope with the death of his parents and brother. She remembered taking his hand and encouraging him that things would get better. The sudden pang in her stomach was as much nostalgia as it was realization that, apparently, things had not gotten better.

Why else would he have gone to Mexico, a place he admittedly loathed? Why else would he want to get away, seemingly going to lengths to avoid those who cared about him? Why else would he . . .

And why else would she be about to follow him there?

*   *   *

Nine days ago . . .
6:03 p.m.

AFTER TALKING to Ashley, Sam showered and changed into jeans and a sweater, fighting against a chilly snap that had come in with October and not, as of yet, lifted. Then she set about making something simple for dinner. She had some leftover chicken in the refrigerator that would mix with a seasoned rice package. With a quickly tossed salad, it would suffice.

Before she could start, her cell rang. She found it on the counter and glanced at the display. It was an unknown number, but she answered it anyhow. "This is Sam."

"Sam," the voice said. It was a woman's, husky, familiar. When she continued, it became apparent why. "This is Maggie, Jack's friend."

"Yeah, Maggie, hi."

"Hey. Say, this is kind of an odd question, but do you have any idea where Jackson is?"

Sam walked to the loveseat and sat down.

"Sam?"

"Yeah, I'm here. Sorry, you're just the second person to call and ask that today."

"Who else is looking for him?"

"Detective Ashley Larson."

"Yeah, Ashley's the one who called me."

"She called you?"

"Yesterday morning," Maggie answered. "She was worried because she hadn't been able to get ahold of him, and said she was calling friends of his."

Sam put out of her mind—for the moment at least—why Ashley had called Maggie a day earlier than she'd called her. It wasn't important right now.

"I told her I hadn't talked to him in over a month," Maggie continued, "but I'd try to get ahold of him. I called him a couple of times, stopped at his house. Nothing. I talked to his neighbor, Connie, who's miffed because he hasn't mowed her lawn since August, but has no idea where he is and hasn't seen him in—her words—'forever.' I stopped in to see Reggie at his restaurant, but he wasn't there. I stopped to see his grandpa. Not there. Gave a call to that P.I. I worked with the last time Jackson went off the grid, Tori Walker, and she's in Barstow on some big case all week but hasn't heard from him. I got your number from the hospital, but I don't suppose you know anything more than anybody else."

"Actually, I do," Sam said.

"Have you talked to him?"

"No."

"But you know something?"

Sam explained, as she had to Ashley an hour ago, about her visit to Reggie after she'd been unable to reach Jackson herself. She didn't tell Maggie why she'd wanted to find Jackson. She wasn't entirely sure herself.

"He went to Mexico?" Maggie asked. "Jackson hates Mexico."

"I know."

"I mean, really bad. After everything that happened there."

"That's right, the two of you were there."

"Yeah, and we left as *personas non grata*, too. He went back there voluntarily?"

"From what Reggie told me."

"Why?"

"I don't know."

"When did you talk to Reggie?"

"A week ago Sunday."

"And you've just been sitting on this?"

Sam leaned forward, trying not to take offense at the critique in Maggie's voice. "Reggie didn't seem worried. There's nothing to suggest Jackson was in trouble."

"Have you talked to him since?"

"No. He's in Nebraska."

"What?"

"He has family there."

"He have a phone there too?"

"Ashley played a little phone tag with him, but sounds like he's hard to reach."

"Yeah, who knows if they even have cell towers in Nebraska."

"Maggie, can I ask you something?"

"Shoot."

"Are you worried about Jackson?"

"I'm getting there. I'm trying to tell myself this isn't like last time, but who knows what's happened to him since he sent Reggie that postcard you mentioned. He might have flipped and gone down there to chill for a few weeks, but it's Mexico. And Jackson. Trouble follows him."

"I know. And it's not like him to be off the grid this long . . ."

"Unless something happened to him?" Maggie finished.

"Yeah."

Maggie sighed.

"You said Leroy was gone too?" Sam asked.

"Yeah, checked his houseboat twice."

"Reggie didn't say anything about him."

"I swear, there's something in the genetics in that family."

Sam said nothing.

"I had a source in Mexico," Maggie said after a while. "She worked at *El Universal* in Mexico City, and her brother-in-law was a detective in Acapulco. One of the few people who didn't burn us when we were down there. I'll give her a call and see if she knows anybody in Tijuana who could . . . I don't know, verify Jackson's not in jail for publicly burning the

Mexican flag or screaming 'Remember the Alamo!' at a soccer match or something. Or on a slab in the morgue."

"You don't really think that, do you?"

"No. But like I told you, I'm worried."

Sam again said nothing. She shared the sentiment.

"I'll give her a call," Maggie said. "I'll keep you posted."

"Thanks. Hey, Maggie?"

"Yeah."

"You think there's any chance he's back and just holed up in the dark playing video games or watching *24* on a loop?"

"No. Connie let me in. House is empty, car's gone, looks unlived in."

Sam sighed.

"I'll keep you posted," Maggie said again, then hung up, leaving Sam to eat a so-so supper while trying to tell herself, just as Maggie had, that this *wasn't* like last time.

Chapter Two

"MAGGIE, ARE YOU sure about this?"

She turned from the passenger seat. "I'm sure, Russell."

"It's just, the last time you were in Mexico, things didn't go so well."

"You're telling me."

"Aren't you wanted by the *federales*?"

"That was Acapulco, not Tijuana," she said, looking out the window at the Santa Monica skyline.

"You trying to convince me or you?" Russell asked.

Maggie looked back at him. "You remember what I told you on Skyler's patio?"

"You mean right before you committed a felony by breaking into his house?"

She set her tongue in her jaw.

"I remember," Russell said. "You said if the situation was reversed, there was nothing Jackson wouldn't do to save you."

She nodded.

"But that was different, Maggie. Back then, we thought he'd been targeted—we thought Skyler had hired somebody to take him out—or he was part of some Grays-Silvaz gang war collateral damage. That's not the case now."

"You don't know that."

"You told me what Reggie said."

Maggie sighed as Russell turned off Ocean Avenue. "Look, I know it's not the same. And I know what Reggie said, but . . ."

11

"You feel you owe him yet."

"It's not that I owe him, Russell. It's that, even with all we've been through and with how we left things, he's still my friend. And he needs help."

"You're sure that's it?"

Maggie swallowed. "That's it."

"Okay."

"Okay?"

Russell nodded. "I don't like it, but I get it. Just promise me you'll be careful."

"Of course."

"You're still my friend too."

She smiled. "I know. There's safety in numbers. And Ashley's a cop. You saw her at Petrovich's place and the hospital. Would you cross her?"

That brought a grin to Russell's unshaven and handsome face. "No I would not."

"I'll be fine."

He nodded resignedly.

"Thanks for the lift."

"Call me when you get back?"

"You got it."

He stuck out a fist, and Maggie banged her knuckles into it. She hoisted a backpack off the floor and opened her door. She turned to wink at Russell. "Later."

He nodded again as she closed the door.

She took a deep breath and started across the pier toward the two blond women standing by the parking area gate.

You're sure that's it?

She ignored Russell's question and her answer and forced an upbeat smile to her face as she nodded at Ashley and Sam.

*　　　　　*　　　　　*

Four days ago . . .
Monday, October 14
6:23 p.m.

"SORRY I'M late," Sam said as she exited the main doors of Santa Monica-UCLA Medical Center.

Maggie stood up, having been leaning against a column that supported a carport that fit at a resort hotel. "Goes with the territory, I imagine," she said, noting Sam's purple hospital scrubs. "You could have changed."

"I figured you were waiting already."

Maggie waved her off.

"My car or yours?" Sam asked.

"My car's a Yamaha motorcycle, so . . ."

"Mine," Sam said with a small laugh.

Maggie was struck with the same observance she'd had talking to Sam on the phone a few times—she was cute. Maggie couldn't put her finger on it, but she could see why Jackson would have been attracted to her— even if she wasn't exactly his type. And evidence seemed to be mounting—Sam being his "nurse" after he got shot, her being vitally interested in his survival when the Russians got ahold of him in the spring, her being one of Ashley's contacts now—that she and Jackson had been, at least on some level, involved.

Maggie followed Sam a block to her car, a blue Ford Fusion. It had been a crazy weekend. In addition to taping several segments for various cable networks about the president's new immigration policy, she'd been working on an initial draft of a speech she'd been asked to give to the journalism department at her alma mater next month, and had fended off several advances from a would-be Romeo who had just moved into her apartment. And that was all on top of wondering about Jackson's voyage to Mexico and waiting to hear back from Mauricio, a beat reporter for *Frontera* in Tijuana and a contact of Maggie's source, Anapaula, with *El Universo* in Mexico City. She'd called Anapaula the previous Thursday, after talking to Sam and Ashley. It'd taken till Friday to get ahold of

Mauricio, and he hadn't gotten back to her until just that morning. Maggie had called Ashley and Sam immediately, prompting her and Sam to seek out Reggie—if he was back from Nebraska—with Ashley waiting anxiously for a report.

The sun was out but the air was cool. From inside Sam's Focus, that didn't matter. The views were great as they cut over to the coast and headed north toward Cameron's, the beachside restaurant owned and operated by Jackson's best friend, Reggie Cameron. An awkward silence pervaded the ride, and Maggie was glad when Sam turned—albeit a little delicately—into the parking lot of Cameron's. They had not called ahead, so it was iffy if Reggie was there and could make time for them if he was, but some things needed to be discussed in person.

A young woman in a skirt and light sweater greeted them when they entered the foyer. Cameron's was an upscale bistro upstairs and a casual, open to the beach café downstairs. It featured something for everyone, and the food was good. At least on Maggie's few visits.

"Just two of you?" the hostess asked. A gold nameplate identified her as Kellyn.

"We're actually here to see Mr. Cameron, if he's available," Maggie said.

"Do you have an appointment?" Kellyn asked, immediately frowning.

"No, but if you could tell him Maggie and Sam are here, I think he'll make time for us."

"Okay, I'll let him know. You can have a seat over there," she said, pointing toward a bench by the window, "or you can wait at the bar if you'd like."

They sat on the bench, and Kellyn reached into her dais for a phone. Her conversation was quiet and clipped, but she announced that Mr. Cameron would be right along. Less than a minute later, he climbed the steps from the basement.

At six-three, two-fifty, arms marked with faded tats and bulging with muscles, Reggie Cameron cut an intimidating figure. He offset it with a grin, usually, but his face was straight as he approached Maggie and Sam. "This can't be good," he said.

"Why's that?" Sam asked.

He dismissed the remark with a wave. "Come down to my office?"

"Thanks," Maggie said.

"You all hungry?"

"No," Maggie said.

Sam shook her head.

"All right, follow me."

He led them downstairs, through the dining room and a hallway, and into his private office looking out on the beach. In addition to a spacious desk and traditional office accoutrements, it featured a full-sized couch and big screen TV, a table and chairs, and a private bathroom. He offered them seats on the couch and spun one of the chairs at the table around, straddling it backward.

"I don't suppose this is because you had a rude waiter or found something suspicious in your salads."

"No," Maggie said.

"I told her what you told me about Jackson," Sam said.

"We need more, Reggie," Maggie said.

He tipped his head to the side. "There ain't more."

"Come on."

Reggie extended his palms. "It's like I told Sam, he said he needed to get away, needed some solitude."

"In Mexico?"

"Doesn't know anybody there, doesn't speak enough Spanish to find a bathroom. I guess he figured that's away."

"He hates Mexico."

Reggie nodded.

"Have you heard anything more from him?" Sam asked.

"Not since the postcard I showed you," he said, cutting his eyes to Maggie.

"She told me."

"I just got back from Nebraska last night, so I've been scrambling to catch up here, but he hasn't called, left me a message. He wasn't crashing on my couch last night." He shrugged. "You check his house?"

"Two hours ago. He's gone."

Another shrug.

"I had a source down in Mexico, from last time," Maggie said. "She put me in touch with a reporter with *Frontera*, who checked the wire. Reggie, Jack was arrested last month. On the fourteenth. That's not long after you said he went down there."

Reggie took the news with a nod. "Arrested for what?"

"Drunk and disorderly conduct at a bullfight."

Reggie nodded again.

"What, that's it?"

"I don't know what you want me to tell you."

"Jackson doesn't drink, Reggie."

"I know that."

"He's always been sober as a judge. But I had Connie let me into his house again today, after I heard from this guy in Tijuana. I looked a little closer than the first time. He had half a case of beer in his refrigerator, a couple folded up boxes in his garage, and a bottle of tequila in his cupboard."

Reggie was blank.

"Then he runs off to Mexico, a place he loathes, a place he wouldn't spit on if it was burning to the ground, and a week after getting there, he's arrested for being drunk and disorderly. And now it's been a month, and nobody's heard from him. And all you've got is a shrug?"

Reggie looked away.

"Did you know about any of this?" Sam asked. "That he was drinking?"

"Yeah," he said softly.

"What?" Maggie asked.

He sighed. "J's been messed up, man. I mean, he's been depressed for a while, but it's been bad lately. Really bad."

Maggie leaned forward, doing her best to control her frustration. "Then what are you doing here?"

"Where should I be?"

"In Mexico. You're his best friend. Go get him."

"He made it pretty clear when he left he didn't want to be got."

"So what?"

"Maggie, I get it, okay. Your response was my response, but . . . J's a grown man."

"A grown man who's throwing his life away."

"Yeah, well, there comes a time sometimes when you have to let somebody go."

Maggie sat back. She turned to Sam, saw the confusion in her eyes too. She turned back. "Are you serious, Reggie?"

"Look, I tried talking to him. Multiple times." He shook his head. "I don't know if I'm too close, I don't know if I'm not close enough, or I don't know if he's just tuned me out, but I might as well have been talking to the wall. There's nothing I could say to change his mind. Nothing I could do to get him out of the funk. And if I drove to Mexico, threw him in the back of my Hummer, and dragged him back here, he'd leave again tomorrow." He exhaled, looking down for nearly a full minute. When he looked up, his voice was thick. "Sometimes, if somebody's bound and determined to wreck themselves . . ." He exhaled again. "Sometimes you gotta let 'em. Sometimes that's the only way they can ever get to a place where they can be fixed."

Maggie's voice matched Reggie's. "And what if he gets wrecked beyond fixing?"

Reggie opened his mouth but said nothing.

"What about his grandpa?" Sam asked, her voice on the edge of breaking too.

"Last I heard, he was in Houston visiting his brother Donny. Been there at least a month."

"Does he know where Jackson is?"

"J said something about telling him, but I don't know."

Maggie looked away, waiting for either the sadness or the anger to win out.

Reggie broke the silence. "I don't like it any better than either of you do, but it's like I said, J's a grown man. We can talk to him, try to persuade him, pray for him. But in the end, he's going to do what he wants to do." He stood. "I'm sorry, but that really is all I know. I gotta get back to work."

Maggie stood too. "Why were you in Nebraska?"

He turned around. "My grandma died."

"I'm sorry," Sam said, also on her feet.

"Thanks."

"Reggie, I don't . . ." Maggie said. "I don't mean to be indelicate, but is it possible your emotions are out of whack and you're not thinking clearly about this?"

He swallowed, then took a non-threatening step toward her. "Yeah, my emotions are out of whack. They've been out of whack for a while, mostly because of Jack. And I've thought through this and analyzed this from every angle and in every frame of mind, and the facts don't change. I'm praying for him constantly, but right now, there's nothing else I can do. I'm sorry, but I have to go."

With that, he turned and left.

Chapter Three

HILLARY MCKENZIE USUALLY enjoyed the drive through Malibu and along the ocean on the Pacific Coast Highway. Today, however, bumper-to-bumper on the 101 and a rollover on Malibu Canyon Road had her feeling frustrated—and in danger of being late. She pushed the accelerator of her Lexus ISC 350 toward the floor and careened around a slow-moving delivery truck.

It wasn't just traffic making her frustrated. It was Jackson. What was he doing in Mexico? And had he really started drinking, after being a teetotaler all his life, after giving her so much flack for an occasional cocktail or glass of wine? Was it possible he was *that* depressed?

Truth be told, Jackson had been frustrating her since day one. They'd met on Memorial Day when Jackson's brother Grant had brought her, his girlfriend of a month, to meet the family. It had been another year and a half before Grant had proposed, but already that Memorial Day Hillary had believed there might be something special between her and Grant, and had been looking forward to meeting his parents and brother. Especially the brother. Hillary had two sisters, and they were great, but she thought a brother-in-law might be nice someday. And Grant couldn't stop talking about his big brother, Jackson.

Hillary's first thought as she rounded the corner was that Grant's big brother—who stood by the grill, twirling a spatula—was kind of cute.

"Hey, Jack," Grant said, climbing onto the deck.

"Grant."

"Jack, this is Hillary."

Hillary extended her hand and looked into cobalt blue eyes. She couldn't identify just what it was about him—his carefree "Hi," his relaxed demeanor, his rugged (at least compared to smooth-shaven Grant) good looks. It was frustrating. She hadn't expected to be attracted to her boyfriend's brother.

"It's nice to meet you," Hillary said, feeling an upturn in the corner of her mouth. She wasn't usually drawn to shaggy hair or scruffy jaws, and while Jackson maybe wasn't cover-boy handsome, he was definitely good-looking. She remembered wondering, as she gave him a finger wave and followed Grant to meet his grandpa, why he didn't have a girlfriend.

She'd found out why throughout the afternoon when Jackson proved, despite his initial allure, to be thoroughly vexing. Cavalier, flippant, disrespectful. What seemed like getting off on the wrong foot had turned into an at times bitter rivalry between the two of them. Jackson never missed a chance to take a dig at her, her chosen profession, her family, or her relationship with Grant. As flummoxing as his logic and his arguments could be, Hillary couldn't deny that somehow, in a twisted, only-Jackson-would-think-of-that sort of way, they kind of made sense too. And no matter how many times she proved herself to him, bested him in a debate, or seemed to parry his verbal thrust, he always squirmed free. As things got serious between her and Grant, Hillary questioned how she and Jackson would ever coexist as family.

That had never happened, of course, because Grant and his parents had been killed two and a half years ago. Hillary had been devastated, but had finally found closure, finally found a way to move forward with her life. Jackson, it seemed, had not.

Empathy was not one of Hillary's stronger suits, and she couldn't understand—his grief notwithstanding—how Jackson could truly be on the brink of throwing his life away, as it sounded like he was. As much bad blood as there was between them, she couldn't stand by and let that happen.

Besides, she owed him. A little more than a year ago, he had saved her life—multiple times. He'd gone to great lengths, risking his life and future for her. His actions still amazed her, and defied everything she'd otherwise believed about him. To this day, she still questioned if for two and a half years she had misjudged him. And if she had once, was it possible she was doing so again?

At any rate, she owed him the benefit of an initial doubt. Why else would she be chasing to Mexico after him?

*　　　　　*　　　　　*

Three days ago . . .
Tuesday, October 15
6:04 p.m.

"I LOVE you too, Brian," Hillary said. She and her fiancé said goodbye, and she tapped her phone to disconnect the call. "Sorry about that," she said as she turned back to her flat-panel computer monitor. The screen was split in four to show everyone on the conference call.

"It's fine," Ashley said from the left frame.

"Now what's with this intervention about Jackson?" Hillary asked.

Ashley took the lead, but Sam and Maggie both took turns as well, filling Hillary in on what they knew about Jackson. He'd been depressed, worse than usual, had started drinking, gone to Mexico—a place he hated—to get away, hadn't made contact with anyone since sending Reggie a glib postcard, wasn't answering phone calls, and had been arrested his first week in Tijuana. Hillary listened with surprise, and yet not shock. This was Jackson, after all. He'd once summoned her to rescue him after he'd been busted smoking marijuana with some lame friends of his. He spent his free time watching '80s TV and playing video games. The drinking was unexpected, as was Mexico, but him wanting to get away from it all—even running away—not so much.

Hillary sat back in her office chair at the prestigious L.A. law firm of Conway, Davenport & Rankin. She had been there for five-plus years and worked her way high enough up the totem pole to have the privacy of her own office. "Look, I admit it's not the happiest news in the world, but I'd have to agree with Reggie. Jackson's a grown man."

Maggie sighed from the screen's middle frame. Sam looked down in the far right frame. Ashley opened her mouth a couple of times but didn't speak. Hillary studied all three women, trying to read them, trying to gauge both the depth of and the reason for their concern for Jackson.

"Hillary," Ashley finally said at length, "I'll ask you the question I've asked myself half a dozen times over the last week. If the roles were reversed, and I was running away, if I was ignoring my friends, drinking myself into oblivion, would he turn his back on me and let me go? Or would he do whatever it took to help me?"

"Me too," Maggie said before Hillary could reply. "Same question I asked back in March when Russian terrorists had him. I knew he'd do whatever it took to save me from them, because he had, and I know he'd go the distance to save me from myself. He did that too."

Hillary licked her lips. "I owe Jackson as much as any of you do. But I don't know what we're supposed to do about it."

"Go get him," Ashley said.

"Get him?"

"Talk some sense into him."

"Jackson and I never talked about his 'love life,' so I don't know what any of your relationships were with him, but do you really think he'll listen to you if he won't listen to his best friend?"

"Collectively, yes," Ashley said.

"According to Reggie, Jackson had tuned him out," Maggie said. "We can be a different voice."

"Assuming that's true, and assuming you can find him, what does that have to do with me? Mine isn't a voice that will sway Jackson."

"I disagree," Sam said quietly. "Hillary, I know you and Jackson weren't close. But deep down, I think he respected you."

Hillary huffed. "Jackson didn't respect me. Just the opposite."

"On the surface, maybe. He covered with a lot of wisecracks and negative comments. But he wouldn't have pushed back against you so much if he didn't ultimately respect you."

"For what it's worth, I agree," Maggie said. "I know what happened in Nevada, Hillary. And I know how he talked about what happened. He wasn't just fulfilling an obligation to his brother's fiancée. He may not have admitted it, but I think like Sam said, deep down, he cared about you."

Hillary sighed.

"I don't know," Ashley said. "I got the feeling he hated your guts. But that could be just what he needs—someone who can be tough with him, someone who intimidates him a little."

"I didn't intimidate Jackson. Nothing ever put him ill at ease."

"There's another reason we need you," Ashley continued. "We don't know what he's been up to for a month. Maybe laying on the beach, maybe holed up drinking in his hotel room, or maybe getting in trouble with the cops again. We've got a nurse, a bulldog investigative reporter—I mean that nicely, Maggie."

Maggie winked at her.

"A cop," Ashley continued. "We could use a good lawyer too. And I'm not flattering you, Hillary, I'm stating facts. You're the best."

"You all are serious?"

"We are."

Sam nodded.

"We're going with or without you," Maggie said. "We'd prefer with you."

"How are you going to find him? He might be in Mexico City by now, or Cancun, or South America for that matter."

Maggie's response was to shrug.

"And what if he won't listen? What if he won't come back? Or can't come back. Mexican authorities aren't going to care much what one detective from California says, nor the courts what one American lawyer says. They imprison people for years for just crossing the border illegally or for other small infractions."

"All the more reason to go get him now, before anything worse happens to him," Sam said.

"Or he does something worse to himself," Ashley said.

"We've got details to work out, no doubt," Maggie said. "Between the three of us—and hopefully four—we can work them out." She shook her head. "But not knowing exactly how we're going to do it isn't going to stop us from doing it."

"Have you talked to Reggie about this plan?"

"Not yet. But he seemed pretty set on letting Jackson work through this himself."

Hillary leaned back in her chair, casting her eyes to the ceiling. Ashley, Maggie, and Sam made some decent points, but that didn't change Hillary's mind that this seemed like an impulsive overreaction. They didn't have a plan to find Jackson, a plan to persuade him to come back, a plan to avoid getting into trouble themselves. Four young, attractive females searching for a depressed, semi-depraved, runaway private investigator in Mexico. What could possibly go wrong?

And yet, Hillary couldn't get Ashley's initial question out of her mind. *If the roles were reversed, would he turn his back on me and let me go? Or would he do whatever it took to help me?*

Hillary knew the answer, knew it firsthand. A year ago, she'd had to beg and cajole Jackson to help her find answers in Las Vegas. Things had gone sideways, and she'd been kidnapped by rogue CIA agents and a paramilitary group conducting insidious experiments at a decommissioned Air Force base in the desert. Jackson had basically staged a *Die Hard* movie to save her. Could she really, with a clear conscience, not take a few days to try to help him?

"Well?" Maggie asked.

Hillary lowered her eyes to make eye contact with Maggie in the webcam. "Two conditions."

"Name them," Ashley said.

"Anybody tries anything crazy, and I'm out. And I mean it. We'll be treading on thin ice, so if any of you dream up some . . . Jackson-like plan to get info from a cute bartender or something, I'm done."

"We'll be a unanimous democracy," Ashley said. "Each with full veto power."

Hillary eyed her for a moment.

"What's the other condition?" Maggie asked.

"We don't drive down to Mexico with no strategy. We figure out a plan of attack and line up any resources we can before we leave."

Ashley and Maggie looked at each other, then both nodded. So did Sam as Ashley said, "Deal. Let's get planning."

Hillary slid her cell phone over and tapped in Brian's number. He answered almost immediately. "Hey, Babe, what's up?"

"Something came up at work," Hillary said evenly. "I'm afraid I'm going to have to take a rain check on tonight."

*   *   *

Friday, October 18
8:01 a.m.

AS HILLARY entered the parking area behind the Carousel on the Santa Monica Pier, she had no problem recognizing her traveling companions. A few rays of sun had peeked out from an otherwise overcast morning, and they seemed to dance off Ashley and Sam's blond hair. In Southern California, blond hair—like Hillary's—was as common as surf and sun. In Mexico, they would stand out like sore thumbs. Between the blondes stood the female version of Jackson, a woman with natural good looks and a carefree disposition, and one who Hillary had learned, like Jackson, didn't hesitate to speak her mind.

Hillary parked and grabbed her duffel and a now lukewarm cup of dark roast coffee, then joined the others. They said good mornings, and Ashley beeped open the rear of a burnt orange Nissan Rogue. Well, that wouldn't stand out, at least. Hillary swung her duffel off her shoulder and into the SUV.

"I don't suppose any of you have happened to hear from Jackson or Reggie or had second thoughts about this trip?" she said after a drink of her coffee. It was past lukewarm, and she set her eyes searching for a trash can.

"No to hearing from anyone, and I'm way past second thoughts," Ashley said.

Hillary raised an eyebrow.

"I did give Mouse a call," Maggie said.

"Who?"

"A friend of Jackson's, a techie guy. Can hack anything."

"To what end?"

She shrugged. "I thought maybe he could hack Jackson's phone or Mexican police records or something."

During several planning discussions, they had thought about calling the Mexican authorities instead of driving all the way down to Tijuana. But Ashley had lobbied for visiting them in person. Mexican cops were known for being corrupt and understaffed, and she figured they'd have a better chance with a live body standing in front of a desk than making calls. Plus, they still had to physically go to get Jackson.

"Did he find anything?" Sam asked.

"Said he couldn't hack in Mexican."

Hillary rolled her eyes.

"And Jack's phone is too old."

"Of course." She spotted a trashcan by the entrance gate and walked her coffee cup to it. As she was returning, she heard the clatter of tires over the pier planks and turned to see a gray Mercedes Benz sedan sweep into the lot. It swept a little too fast, caroming into a parking spot a few down from the Rogue. Hillary looked at the other three women. Only a handful of cars dotted the parking area, given the early hour, and the pier was all but deserted except for fishermen. People who fished off the pier didn't drive Mercedes Benz sedans.

"We didn't invite a fifth wheel, did we?"

"No," Maggie said with some hesitation. She turned toward the sedan, and Hillary's eyes followed. A ball of coiffed hair the color of Lucille Ball's popped over the roof, followed by a brightly colored—and there were too many colors to pick just one—wrap of some kind. A poncho or serape? The woman was tall and heavy, and as she removed enormous wraparound sunglasses from her face, Hillary saw she was wearing enough makeup for an entire mime troop. Bright and gaudy makeup. A street performer arriving early? Not in a Benz.

She waved, which was disconcerting, then opened the back door of the sedan. A moment later, she came around the rear pulling a rolling suitcase behind her—more like dragging it across the pier—and balancing two large Tupperware containers on top of an insulated casserole dish in the other. She walked right up to the edge of the group and stopped.

"Oh thank heavens," she said. "I was afraid you'd have left already, and my sticky buns took forever to rise this morning."

"Connie?" Sam frowned. She stepped forward to take the precariously balanced Tupperware containers.

"Thank you, dear."

"What are you doing here?" Maggie asked.

"And I'm sorry, but who are you?" Hillary asked.

"This is Jackson's neighbor, Connie," Sam said.

"I don't believe we've met," she said, letting go of her rolling suitcase and extending a hand—brightly ornamented with lime green nail polish— the one color not in her garment.

"Hillary McKenzie."

"Oh," she said with obvious surprise. "You're Hillary."

Hillary forced a thin-lipped grin.

"Connie, what are you doing here?" Maggie asked again.

"Isn't it obvious? I'm going with you to find Jackson. As they say down there, *c'est la vie!*"

Chapter Four

CONNIE SAT ON the hump in the backseat of the Rogue, which rode like a lumber wagon compared to her Mercedes. She served her special homemade sticky buns, on Corelle pie plates with actual silverware, while Ashley drove them first east on Interstate 10, then south on the 405. The clouds had not broken, and it was a mostly gloomy morning, made even gloomier by the elevator music Hillary had tuned in on the radio.

Connie focused on learning about her traveling companions, none of whom she knew very well. Jackson had always been so secretive about his harem. "Have any of you ever been to Mexico before?" she asked.

"Once," Maggie said.

"Which part?"

"Acapulco."

"Oh, that's lovely. My first husband and I visited Acapulco back in 1991 or '92. No, that must have been my second husband. We had a lovely time there. Did you enjoy it?"

"Well, I spent most of my time trying not to get killed by a crooked oil tycoon, so . . ."

"Oh, that's right. Jackson had to come save your life, didn't he?"

"For the first time."

"These are delicious," Sam said from Connie's other side.

"Thank you, Samantha." Connie leaned forward. "Ashley, Hillary?"

"Sorry, I can't eat while driving," Ashley said.

"No, I mean have you ever been to Mexico?"

"No," she said.

"Cancun, a long time ago," Hillary said.

Connie sat back. "I wish I spoke more Spanish."

"How much do you speak?" Sam asked.

"*Nada*. But I know some Italian. They're very similar languages."

"How do you know if you don't speak Spanish?" Ashley asked with a wink in the rearview mirror.

"Well, I brought along a travel guide," Connie said, swinging her purse off her shoulder and digging through it. "I think it has some basic translation."

"We all know enough Spanish to be conversant," Ashley said.

Connie stopped digging. "Does Jackson know Spanish?"

"Not a lick," Maggie said.

"Then how in the world is he making his way down there?"

"I think the bottoms-up gesture is pretty universal," Hillary muttered. Connie tisked.

"What's in the Tupperwares?" Sam asked.

Connie spent the next fifteen minutes telling her about the muffins and cookies she had baked—original family recipes both. By that time, they were past the airport, making fairly good progress in L.A.'s notoriously bad traffic.

"Can I ask you something?" Maggie said as Connie served her a second sticky bun. "They are great, by the way."

"Thank you, and of course."

"When was the last time you talked to Jackson?"

"Oh good heavens, let me think. Well, he mowed my lawn the day after Labor Day. It had rained most of that weekend, so it was quite long. He always lets it get so long. And then . . . I waved to him a day or two later and shouted hello, but that was it. I didn't think much of it, he'd been gone so much of late, but after a few weeks, I realized I hadn't seen him since that day. I thought maybe he was on a case or had finally gotten some sense and swept one of you ladies off your feet and taken you to Paris or something. Or I should say, back to Paris," she said, nudging Maggie.

"We never wen—"

"He never said anything to me about going to Mexico."

"Did he say anything?" Ashley asked.

"Not very much. He seemed particularly depressed. Jackson never was the most upbeat of persons, but the last few months had been really bad."

"Since when?" Ashley asked.

"Hmm . . . Ever since he got back from Florida."

"Jackson was in Florida?" Sam asked.

"Back in May."

"Why?"

"I think he said something about visiting an old friend."

"Hmm."

"But I'd say about the last couple of months he's been distant. I'd seen him less and less, until not at all. Didn't see either of you two ladies either," she said, turning her eyes from Maggie to Sam and back. Neither of them said anything.

"Hillary, when was the last time you talked to him?" Ashley asked.

"The Sunday after Labor Day. And it was weird."

"How so?"

"He called me up out of the blue, asked if we could meet, and begged me not to marry my fiancé."

"You're engaged?"

Hillary nodded.

"You're not wearing a ring."

"I didn't want to give anyone a target in Mexico."

"Weren't you engaged to Jackson's brother?" Connie asked.

"I was."

"You think that's why Jack didn't want you to get married again?" Ashley asked.

"Who knows with him? He wouldn't tell me."

"Maybe he wanted you for himself," Connie said.

Hillary couldn't keep a derisive laugh from escaping her mouth.

"How did he seem to you then?" Maggie asked.

Hillary looked back. "Half dead."

Maggie frowned.

"Half dead?" Connie asked.

Hillary sighed. "As if his soul had died but his body didn't know enough to fall over. It was scary."

"And you didn't say anything?" Sam asked.

"To whom?"

Nobody had an answer.

"I saw him end of August," Maggie said after almost a minute. "He, um . . . wanted to apologize for being a little out of sorts last time we'd seen each other."

"Jackson apologized for that?" Hillary asked.

"I'll never forget the look in his eyes. I couldn't place it until you just said that, Hillary, but it was as if he was dead inside."

"Did you tell anyone?" Connie asked.

"No. Unfortunately, it was a growingly familiar look."

"I saw him in passing at church a few times, probably back in June or July," Sam said. "But I haven't said more than hi in the church hallway since back in April."

"This is so peculiar," Connie said.

"Man, this really is starting to feel like last time," Maggie said.

"Last time?" Connie asked.

"The Russians."

"What exactly happened?" Hillary asked.

"You didn't hear about that?" Ashley said.

"Just bits and pieces from what you've mentioned the last few days. But I never got the whole story."

"Jackson disappeared out of the blue back in March. Didn't answer anybody's calls, wasn't at home, hadn't said anything about going to Mexico or sent any postcards. Turns out he was kidnapped by Chechen terrorists. He was working for a retired U.S. Army vet who knew secrets about Nazi nuclear warheads from his service in World War II. He was the last of his unit, the last to know what he knew, and this Chechen terrorist cell wanted to get its hands on the nukes. So they grabbed Jackson in an effort to find Wilbur—this vet—and tortured him for intel."

Hillary's eyes widened. "Tortured him?"

"Half killed him. I mean they beat the ever-loving crap out of him."

"I had no idea."

"Most of the details didn't make the papers," Ashley said. "For obvious reasons."

"So you all found him and rescued him?" Hillary asked.

Ashley nodded. "Us, Reggie, Leroy, Mouse, an old P.I. friend of his. Pretty much anybody who knew or cared about him."

Hillary looked out her window. "How bad was it?"

"Bad," Maggie said. "He said it got so bad, toward the end, he started egging them on, hoping they'd finish him off."

"My goodness," Connie said, crossing herself. Then she looked toward Maggie. "You don't think . . ."

"What, that Jack's suicidal?"

"I don't want to say it."

"Jackson wouldn't kill himself," Hillary said.

"What makes you say that?" Ashley asked.

"Because if he was going to, he would have by now."

"Maybe he wouldn't kill himself," Maggie said, "but he might not keep living, either. You know how when some old people lose a spouse they quit eating, stop trying to live? Sort of like the old animal that wanders off in the field to die."

"That's lovely," Hillary said.

Maggie shrugged.

"You think that's what this is?" Connie asked. "Jackson went down to Mexico to die?"

"Maybe not so overtly," Maggie said. "Maybe not even consciously. But Reggie said he wanted to get away. Maybe he just doesn't want to go on anymore, and this is his way of . . . I don't know."

"Jackson wouldn't do that," Sam said. "I can't believe it."

"I agree," Ashley said. "But even if he would, we're not going to let that happen."

As if to punctuate her thought, she switched lanes and accelerated past an old pickup truck plastered full of redneck bumper stickers. She kept accelerating, taking dead aim for the Mexican border.

*   *   *

10:22 a.m.

THE GROUP stopped just south of San Diego to top off the gas tank, use the restrooms, and stretch. Then they loaded back into the Rogue and headed for the border. Already, traffic was beginning to back up, and Ashley strummed her fingers impatiently on the wheel while waiting. She didn't know why—it wasn't like another thirty minutes or an hour was going to make a big difference, what with Jackson having been in country for over a month. But their talks about depression and suicide had started to strike a chord with her, and she was anxious to find him and see how bad he really was. She still hoped maybe they were overreacting, and Jackson was just enjoying an extended vacation. There was an excuse for the liquor in his house, for the arrest Maggie's source's contact had learned about. This was all just a misunderstanding, and by sunset the five of them would be sitting around a table of fajitas with Jackson laughing about old times.

Yeah right.

The San Ysidro Port of Entry saw more than seventy thousand vehicular border crossings per day, but moved the five women through in reasonably short order. Ashley hadn't been sure about bringing food— Connie's leftover sticky buns, muffins, and cookies—into Mexico. Border guards and custom agents were sticklers about that sort of thing sometimes, but there was no issue. Nor did her Redding P.D. detective's badge hinder or hasten the process. Shortly after eleven-thirty, they were safely into Mexico and headed south on a highway that was the continuation of Interstate 5.

Immediately, everything had changed. Not just the signs and billboards being now in Spanish instead of English. The buildings were from several decades ago but appeared as if they had been in place for centuries, in various stages of neglect and disrepair. Everything was dirty and grimy. L.A. had plenty of neighborhoods—Redding even had some— that would never make the chamber of commerce's website, but this took it to an entirely new level.

"You didn't bring your gun, huh?" Maggie asked from the front seat, having swapped with Hillary.

"Why, nervous already?" Hillary asked from the back.

"No, not after last time. I was just thinking having seen her badge."

"No, I didn't," Ashley said. "Thought that might be more trouble than it's worth. And if it comes to needing it . . ."

"I thought maybe you thought you might have to herd Jackson back at gunpoint."

Ashley raised one eyebrow at Maggie, looking to see if she was serious or not. Not, she was pretty sure. "You want to help me with directions?" she said.

"Yeah, sure," Maggie said, sitting up and retrieving several city maps and directions to the police headquarters that Ashley had printed off the night before. The Mexican legal system was a little different than in the U.S. There were the federal authorities—a.k.a. the *federales*—who oversaw major crimes like trafficking, drug enforcement, and etcetera. Then each of Mexico's thirty-one states had their own state government and police force. Municipalities had police departments too, but they handled minor infractions—mostly traffic related. Ashley didn't know where drunken disorderly conduct at a bullfight fell on the scale, but she guessed it didn't rise to the level of a state offense.

The Tijuana Municipal Police Department was located a block from the Tijuana River, less than a mile from the border. Ashley parked in a small lot, and the five got out. The clouds had broken, leaving a hazy, smoggy, warm sun beating down on Tijuana. On TV, Ashley had noticed any scenes set in Mexico were always filmed with a yellow filter—same for scenes in Africa. There was no yellow tint, but everything seemed washed out. Maybe that was because of the haze, or maybe because of age and decay.

"Okay, who wants to play bad cop?" Ashley asked.

"Don't all look at me," Hillary said.

"Are we really going to waltz in there, all five of us?" Maggie asked.

"You volunteering to stay behind?" Ashley asked.

Maggie said nothing.

"Do we need a bad cop?" Sam asked.

"I'm not running game," Ashley said, cutting off an early veto from Hillary. "No Jackson angle. Just the truth. And no waltzing."

They followed her inside, where the temperature was a little cooler, but not much. A single man in a navy blue uniform stood behind an information desk. Ashley approached it. *"Buenos días, Oficial Peña,"* Ashley said, reading the man's nametag. He was short and wiry, featuring jet black hair and a mustache. A stereotypical Mexican police officer, direct from central casting.

"Buenos días."

"¿Habla Inglés?"

"Yes, I speak English."

"I'm Detective Ashley Larson," she said, displaying her badge. "I'm with the Redding Police Department, in Redding, California. We're looking for this man, Jackson Douglas," she said, holding up her phone with a picture of Jackson on the display. "We understand he was arrested by your department about a month ago."

Officer Peña's eyes swept over the five women. Ashley wore blue jeans and a flannel shirt over a tank top, which didn't look like a cop, unless it was the remake of *Hawaii Five-0*. But aside from Hillary, whose jeans were designer and whose blouse was a step above casual, none of them resembled law enforcement in the least. Most especially Connie.

Peña studied the badge and seemed to accept its authenticity. Then he studied the picture of Jackson. "I do not recognize the face, or the name."

"I believe it was on September 14," Ashley said. "Something about disorderly conduct at a bullfight."

"I am sorry, Detective Larson, but I do not recall."

"Could you please check your arrest records, see if you have any information? All we know is what I told you."

"We are very busy this morning, Detective. And as you said, this arrest is over a month old."

Hillary had stepped forward, perhaps to flirt, perhaps to threaten a lawsuit. From beside Ashley, she turned and looked over the vacant— save for one person—waiting room. She turned back to Peña, raising her eyebrows.

"Please," Ashley said. "It should only take a few minutes, and it is very important that we find Mr. Douglas." She smiled as sweetly as she possibly could, and tucked a strand of blond hair behind her ear. Funny, she thought to herself, if Jackson was here, he'd probably have enticed her to try the same technique—flirt a little with the Mexican cop.

Whether it was the subtle gesture, the smile, or the sensibleness of her request—or the menacing scowl on Hillary's face—Officer Peña consented. He turned to an older model computer on the desk and typed something into it. He waited nearly thirty seconds, then made several mouse clicks. "Here we go, Jackson Douglas. Age thirty-one, six-foot, two hundred pounds, blond hair, blue eyes."

"That's him."

"He was arrested about nine o'clock on Saturday, September 14, at *Plaza Monumental de Tijuana*. Charge was public intoxication and disorderly conduct."

"What happened?"

"I do not know all the details, but according to the notes here, there was a fight in the stands at a bullfight. We arrested half a dozen individuals. Mr. Douglas was among them."

"And he was drunk?" Maggie asked

"Yes. Slurred speech, unsteady on his feet, he had several lacerations and bruises on his face but was clearly feeling no pain, and he reeked of beer."

"Did you give him a breathalyzer?" Ashley asked. "Do you know what his blood alcohol content was?"

"No. The whole group was clearly drunk, and whether they were or not, they were all disorderly."

"What did you do with him?"

He checked the screen again. "He was thrown in jail for the weekend and was released on Monday morning."

"When is his trial?" Hillary asked.

"There will be no trial, *señorita*. Public intoxication is a small offense, and we have—how you say—bigger fish to fry."

"Do you know anything about where he went when he was released?" Ashley said. "Did he give an address where he was staying?"

"Let me check." Peña turned back to the screen. "*El Hotel Pacífico*."

"Where is that?"

"I am not sure. There's no address. I would guess in the *Playas de Tijuana* borough."

"Is there anything else you can tell us?" Ashley asked. "Names of those he was arrested with, is he in the system again, anything?"

"No, I am afraid I cannot reveal the others' names. And this is all I see on the file."

"What about the arresting officers? Could we speak to them?"

"*Sí*, if you can find them. Officer Franco has not shown up for the last three days and . . ." He consulted the screen again. "Officer Menéndez is vacationing in Nogales through the end of the weekend."

"Is it common for officers not to show up?"

"It is not common, but there are many reasons."

"Likely not tied to an arrest at a bullring a month ago," Maggie muttered.

Ashley nodded. "Okay. Thank you, Officer Peña."

"You are welcome."

The five turned and exited the station. Back outside in the parking lot, they stopped.

"Well, now what?" Connie asked. "Go to this Hotel Pacífico?"

"Worth a try," Hillary said.

"Why would Jackson be at a bullfight?" Maggie asked.

"Is that what it was?" Connie asked. "What did he call it, the Monumental Plaza or something?"

"*Plaza Monumental de Tijuana,*" Ashley said. "It's a bullring by the border."

"And why would he get in a fight?" Maggie asked.

"He probably insulted their national pastime," Hillary said.

Ashley turned to Sam. "You're quiet."

"I just can't believe Jackson was drunk."

"Even with the beer and tequila at his house?" Maggie said.

"Even so. He wouldn't do that."

"Wouldn't he?" Hillary asked.

"I know about the marijuana," Sam said.

"Yeah, well I saw it."

"Jackson smoked marijuana?" Connie asked.

"One joint, once," Ashley said.

"About three months after Grant and his parents died," Hillary said. "He called me up in the middle of the night, said he'd been run in for possession with intent to sell. Begged me to get him off. Said he wasn't selling, just smoking. I got to the station and he was sitting there with a busted lip because he, in his altered state, decided to start a fight with the biggest and baddest guy in the joint. So, yeah, he might just do this."

"We don't know enough yet," Ashley said, trying to calm tensions. "Let's find *El Hotel Pacífico*. With any luck, he'll be there and we can find out from him just what happened."

Chapter Five

EL HOTEL PACÍFICO was located right on the coast, about a thirty-minute drive from the police headquarters. It was a five-story structure from the 1980s, white stucco that was streaked with rust under the windows and by the downspouts descending from a clay-tile roof. Shaped like a flattened V, with the point facing the street and featuring a simple carport, the hotel was surrounded by low, overgrown, uncared for landscaping and a few lazy palm trees. There was a supermarket across the street, a café and—of all things—a pizza restaurant on the same block. The rest of the structures were homes crammed tightly together, dirt driveways, parking lots, and yards between and around them. The street was paved, with a curb and storm drains. The sidewalk was paved too. Telephone poles doubled as streetlights. The neighborhood was a mix, half at least semi-modern, half rundown third-world. That appeared to be the condition of the hotel too.

After parking in a tiny lot south of the carport, Ashley led the way under the carport and into the lobby of *El Hotel Pacífico*. It was not air-conditioned, but open doors and windows let plenty of ocean breeze blow through. The reception desk was on the left of the lobby, with a bar and lounge on the right. Sam looked, almost out of dread, to see if Jackson happened to be slumped on a stool stirring amber liquid in a glass. He wasn't there. Neither was anyone else.

Straight ahead, two pair of sliding glass doors were open to a pool deck and a small but inviting kidney-shaped pool. The deck was surrounded by palms, beyond which was a panoramic view of the Pacific

Ocean. Maybe not the nicest property on Tijuana, but Sam could see the appeal—especially to Jackson.

Ashley asked the young man at the front desk the same question she had asked Officer Peña: *"¿Habla Inglés?"*

"Un poco."

She proceeded to ask him, in Spanish, if they had a man name Jackson Douglas staying at the hotel.

"Jackson Douglas? Let me check." He consulted a computer recessed under the desk. "No, I am sorry, we do not."

"We believe he was here back in September. Can you check and see if that's true, and how long he was here?"

"One moment."

He typed some more, then looked up. "Yes, he was here from the tenth of September through the eighteenth."

"Do you know why he left?"

A woman in a cream blazer over a red silk blouse stepped from a doorway behind the reception desk. She had long, jet black hair and a polite if perfunctory smile. "My name is Gloria," she said in accented but clear English, "and I am the manager of *El Hotel Pacífico*. Thank you, Armando."

The man nodded and stepped aside.

"What is your interest in *Señor* Douglas?"

Ashley pulled out her badge. "I'm a detective from Redding, California," she said. "Jackson Douglas is a friend of ours, and we're trying to find him."

"He is a friend of yours?"

She nodded.

"Then I am sorry to tell you that *Señor* Douglas was asked to leave our hotel."

"Why?" Maggie asked from Ashley's left.

"Because he was causing trouble."

"What kind of trouble?" Hillary asked.

"Several nights after he arrived, we received complaints from multiple guests. He was playing excessively loud music and had rudely spoken to one guest who asked him to turn it down. He was apparently under the influence of alcohol."

"Apparently?" Ashley asked.

"He answered the door with a half-empty bottle of tequila in his hand and nearly fell over."

"Did you speak to him?"

"No, I was not on duty at the time."

"You said that was several nights after he arrived," Hillary said. "Is that when you asked him to leave?"

"No. The night before he left—the seventeenth—we received another complaint. Several of them, in fact. *Señor* Douglas was partying by the pool, after hours, very loud, again clearly drinking too much."

"Partying?" Sam asked from behind Ashley.

"Yes."

"By himself?"

"No, there were several young ladies with him. A couple visitors and one, ah . . . local girl."

"A prostitute?" Hillary asked.

Gloria nodded. "She was escorted from the premises, and the other guests were instructed to leave the pool. In the morning, I personally told *Señor* Douglas that he was no longer welcome at our hotel."

"And he left?" Ashley asked.

"Not immediately. He tried to argue with me, but a police officer happened to be on patrol in the area, and that persuaded him to move on."

"Do you have any idea where he went from here?" Maggie asked. "Did he leave a forwarding address?"

"He did not, no."

"Is there anything else you can tell us?" Connie asked.

"He did run up a rather large bar tab, which he was forced to pay before he left. Other than that, I am afraid not. You could speak with the maid who serviced his room or with Manny, who runs our tiki bar by the pool. I am sure he interacted with him."

"Why are you sure?"

"Because it is my understanding that *Señor* Douglas spent most of his time sitting by the pool and, ah, leering at the female guests."

Sam was getting sick to her stomach. She couldn't believe what she was hearing about Jackson, but what was making her sicker than anything was that a small part of her *did* believe it.

Gloria paged Lenore, the maid who had serviced Jackson's room. Sam and Hillary waited to speak to her, while Ashley, Connie, and Maggie went to talk to Manny. While waiting for Lenore, Sam and Hillary walked through the lobby. Wicker chairs were arranged around potted ferns to form several seating areas. Slow-moving white ceiling fans helped circulate the air blowing in off the pool deck. With the bar backed by a large mirror, it reminded Sam of a scene from an old Bogart movie. She used to make Jackson sit on her loveseat and watch them with her. Not that he minded too much, especially if she plied him with desserts, she thought with a smile. He just couldn't be doing all she was hearing about him.

"Perdóneme. Yo soy Lenore."

Sam and Hillary turned to see a short, somewhat rotund woman in a gray maid's dress. Her silvery black hair was tied into a tight bun, which also pulled any wrinkles out of her face. Her eyes were wide, perhaps with nervousness, but also with kindness, Sam thought. She motioned to one of the seating areas, and the three of them sat down.

"Thank you for your time," Hillary said in Spanish. "We'll be brief."

"Miss Gloria said you wanted to talk about Mr. Douglas?"

"That's right. We understand you were the one who took care of his room?"

"Yes, but only once."

"Only once?" Sam asked.

"He put the 'do not disturb' sign out the first night he was here. I do not work Sundays, but every other day, the sign was up."

"So you only serviced the room when he checked out?" Hillary asked.

"Yes."

"Did you find anything to tell you where he went next?"

Lenore thought for a moment. "No, I do not believe so."

"It was a long shot," Hillary said to Sam. Then to Lenore, "Did he leave anything behind?"

"No. Uh, that is, except for his trash."

"Trash?"

"A lot of food containers, some bathroom supplies, and a lot of liquor bottles."

"Liquor bottles?" Hillary asked.

"Yes."

"From the bar here?" Sam asked.

"No, from a place called Brisa Licores, several blocks away. I recognized their label. They sell very cheap." She looked around. "Cheaper than the hotel bar."

"Figures," Hillary muttered. "Did you find any sign of a woman in his room?"

Lenore frowned. "No, I can't say that I did."

"Anything else that struck you as odd?"

"No, nothing."

"Okay, thank you very much."

Lenore nodded and smiled, then stood to leave. Hillary was about to get up too when Sam reached out a hand to stop her. "Why did you ask her about a woman?"

"Gloria said he was partying with various women at the pool."

"And you assumed he took one of them back to his room?"

"I didn't assume anything. But I wanted to eliminate the worst-case scenario."

"Do you honestly think Jackson would hire a prostitute?"

Hillary looked down.

Sam waited.

"No, I don't. Not a sober Jackson thinking clearly."

Sam didn't like what Hillary left unsaid.

"You can look at me with those accusing eyes all you want," Hillary said.

"I wasn't accusing."

"If you say so. But the fact is, the only reason any of us is down here in the first place is because we're all afraid that Jackson's no longer himself, that he's not making decisions we want him to make or behaving the way we'd expect him to. That doesn't mean he's abandoned every principle he's ever had, but it does mean nothing's off the table. And that's why I asked."

Hillary sent Sam a look that made her understand why Jackson called her the Ice Queen. But, unfortunately, everything she'd just said made perfect sense.

*   *   *

1:04 p.m.

MAGGIE FOUND the pool deck at *El Hotel Pacífico* kind of appealing. It wasn't the rooftop pool at London West Hollywood but, under different circumstances, she could actually enjoy a long weekend lounging around the pool, listening to the Latino music coming from speakers flanking a small tiki bar, maybe enjoying a cocktail or two. The view sure was something, even with the haze.

A dozen or so chaise lounge chairs were spread out on the near side of the pool, with a couple of tables under umbrellas on the right, opposite the tiki bar. Only two of the lounge chairs were occupied, one by a semi-old man in far too short swim trunks reading a novel from behind sunglasses and a hat, and one by a young woman in a bikini. Both were Latino.

Ashley led the way to the bar, where a man in a Hawaiian shirt and a Los Angeles Dodgers baseball cap was—prosaically enough—polishing glasses. "Ah, good afternoon, *señoritas*," he said with a smile full of teeth—one of which was gold. He sounded more like an American with a Spanish accent than the other way around, and his skin could have passed for white with a good tan. "What can I get for you?" he asked.

Smooth as if she'd done it a dozen times—and she probably had—Ashley slapped a twenty-dollar bill on the bar. "Information."

"Information?"

"Are you Manny?"

"Yes."

"Manny, I'm Ashley. This is Maggie and Connie."

"Hello," Connie said.

Maggie waved.

"Are you guests at the hotel?" Manny asked.

"No, but we wanted to ask you about a guest. Gloria said you might be able to help us."

"If Gloria okayed it, sure. Which guest?"

"The one who gave you that hat," Maggie said.

His eyes went up to the brim. "How did you know?"

"I'm the one who made the small stain on the brim. Mustard from a Dodger Dog."

"*Señor* Douglas gave me the hat. He said mine was embarrassing."

"You had a Dodgers hat already?"

"No, *señorita*, a Padres hat."

"You knew *Señor* Douglas well?" Ashley asked.

Manny nodded. "He was by the pool most afternoons. Some mornings too." He chuckled. "And nights."

"What did he do?"

"Flirted with girls. Bought beer."

"From you?"

Manny nodded again.

"He get anywhere with any of the girls?" Maggie asked.

"Not really. I don't think he was trying."

"What do you mean?" Connie asked.

"I think he enjoyed the flirting, you know? I don't think he had any intention of getting serious with any of them."

Maggie raised an eyebrow.

"He cause any trouble?" Ashley asked.

"No, not that I saw." Manny looked toward the entrance to the hotel. "I know he was asked to leave, but I didn't think he was out of line. He and a couple of girls were horsing around. It was after eleven o'clock, and a couple guests were upset. But it's Tijuana, right? People come here to have a little fun."

"What do you mean by horsing around?" Ashley asked.

"He threw one of them in the pool, then they were dunking each other, you know. Chicken-fighting. And he bought them all the booze they could drink. And he tipped well."

Connie muttered something under her breath, half English, half Italian.

"Did you talk to him much, other than about drink orders?" Ashley asked.

"Yeah, we talked baseball. A little soccer."

"Jack talked soccer?" Maggie asked.

"Listened, mostly," Manny said with a smile.

"Anything else?" Ashley asked. "He tell you about his life back home, why he was in Mexico, where he might be going next?"

"No," Manny said, removing the Dodgers hat to ruffle his bushy black hair. "I just assumed he was here to party, you know. He didn't talk about back home at all. Maybe he was running away."

Maggie exchanged glances with Ashley.

"He didn't say where he was going next?" Connie asked.

"Last I talked to him, he wasn't planning on leaving."

"When was that?"

"The night before he left."

"The night he got in trouble for partying?" Ashley asked.

"Yes." Manny snapped. "Oh, there was one other thing. First day or two he was here, he asked me about the fights at Bullring by the Sea."

"What'd he ask?"

"Where he could place a bet."

"On the bullfight?" Maggie asked. "What'd you tell him?"

Manny shrugged. "Bets are easy. There are casinos, betting parlors, private bookies, and lots of informal wagering at the fights."

"Anything else?"

"No, not that I remember."

"Thanks," Ashley said.

"Hey, you sure you *señoritas* don't want something to drink?"

"Maybe later," she said, and they turned to head back inside.

"You know what's funny?" Maggie said.

"What's that?"

"There was a time not too long ago when I would have tried to coerce Jack into the sort of 'party' he threw that night."

"Is that right?"

Maggie nodded. "Never could get him to go along with the idea." She took a look back at the pool before they re-entered the lobby. "Sure makes you wonder what changed."

Chapter Six

AFTER A LATE lunch at a nearby cantina recommended by Gloria, the five women split up. Hillary and Ashley took the Rogue and headed back to the Tijuana Municipal Police Department, hoping this time to talk to someone higher up the food chain. Jackson was no longer at *El Hotel Pacífico*, perhaps not even in Tijuana. Ashley hoped the authorities could put out a BOLO for him or his vehicle. Without it, they were at a dead end. Hillary was tagging along because A) as a lawyer she had experience with the police, B) she had a bulldog demeanor (Jackson's words, according to Maggie) to get the job done, and C) she was hottest if it came to batting eyelashes. That had been Ashley's rather blunt assessment, and nobody had argued. Hillary figured if it came to eyelash batting, they were already out of luck.

The other three, meanwhile, were going to take a taxi to *Plaza Monumental de Tijuana*, also known as Bullring by the Sea. That was where Jackson's legal troubles had originated, and they hoped to learn something from a ticket agent, bookie, fight manager, or whoever might be on duty at a bullring in the middle of the afternoon.

Hillary watched Tijuana go by out her window. At times she felt like she was looking at footage from Falluja or Kandahar. At other times, the views were spectacular, particularly when she looked out Ashley's window. San Diego was visible in the distance, through the haze, and they drove almost to the border wall before curving back into the heart of the city.

Ashley didn't say much, and Hillary wasn't sure if that was concern for Jackson or lack of knowing what to say. Or maybe because she was trying to figure out what to tell her fiancé if he called. Then again, Hillary reasoned, maybe she'd actually told hers where she was going.

"When's your wedding?" Ashley asked

Hillary looked at her sharply.

"Wrong question?" Ashley asked.

"No, sorry, just thinking about something. We haven't set a date yet."

"How long have you been engaged?"

"Late spring."

Ashley nodded.

"What?"

"Nothing."

Hillary turned her head back out her window. "It's okay, ask it."

"I don't have a question."

"You wondered before why Jackson didn't want me to get married."

Ashley nodded.

"He didn't come right out and say why, but he has accused me of moving on too quickly, not caring about Grant."

"That was my question."

"You said you didn't have one."

"I don't."

"You sound like some of the witnesses I come across."

"If I were one of your witnesses, I'd be lying on the floor sucking my thumb, at least to hear Jackson say it."

"I'd rather not hear anything he has to say about it." Hillary exhaled. "What is the question you don't have?"

"How do you know if it's too soon? I'm not saying it is, but . . ."

"I wasn't sure either, for a while. Brian and I took it slow. When I stopped wondering if it was too soon, I knew it wasn't."

"I suppose that makes sense."

Ashley turned her attention to traffic for a while, navigating a cloverleaf onto the highway.

"When's your wedding?" Hillary asked.

"Two weeks from tomorrow."

"Are you serious?"

Ashley turned and smiled sheepishly.

"Jackson must mean quite a bit to you to be down here two weeks before your wedding."

"He does. And it's like I said, he'd do the same for me."

Hillary huffed.

"What?"

"I was going to make a crack about Jackson chasing after an attractive blonde two weeks before his wedding, but then I realized he'll never settle down with just one woman."

Ashley said nothing further, and they drove the rest of the way in silence, other than for a brief discussion about the route. Officer Peña was not working the desk when they arrived, and Ashley took advantage of the fact. She flashed her badge and told the officer at the desk she needed to speak to a detective about an American criminal believed to be in Mexico. The officer asked them to have a seat, and they did.

"An American criminal?" Hillary asked.

"Last time he was here, he broke any number of Mexican laws," Ashley said with a shrug. "That makes him a criminal, and he is American."

"Really?"

Ashley shrugged.

"And you're going to tell the detective that?"

"No. I'm going to tell him just enough actual facts to let him draw his own conclusions."

They sat silently again until a heavyset man in a rumpled suit waddled into the waiting room. He had wavy gray hair and a goatee. His tie was half undone. An old coffee stain marred his off-white shirt. "I'm Detective Zendejas," he said.

"Detective Larson. This is Hillary McKenzie."

They shook hands.

"Come with me, please."

He led them back to a cubicle in a bullpen, not dissimilar from some of the detectives' bullpens Hillary had seen in the U.S.—on 1990s TV shows. Detective Zendejas offered them chairs in front of a Formica desk littered with papers. Zendejas made no effort to clear off any space, merely sat back and crossed his hands over his lap. "What can I do for you ladies?"

Ashley flashed her badge again. "We're looking for Jackson Douglas, an American citizen we believe is here in Tijuana. In fact, we know he was as of one month ago."

"And you said he was a criminal?"

"Yes, sir. He has a history of drug smuggling and also illegally crossing the border."

"Is he in Mexico illegally?"

"No, we believe he's here legally this time. In fact, we think he drove his car. We're hoping you could put out an APB or BOLO for him and his vehicle."

Zendejas sat farther back in his chair. "This drug smuggling—into the United States, I presume?"

"Entirely within, actually," Ashley said. "As far as we know, he has committed no crime in Mexico. Well," she looked to Hillary, "that's not entirely true. He was arrested on September 14 for public intoxication and disorderly conduct at Bullring by the Sea. He also got evicted from *El Hotel Pacífico* for similar behavior."

"So you are looking to have him extradited?"

"Well, that's up to the Mexican government," Ashley said. "We're really just hoping to find him, hoping we can persuade him to come back peacefully."

"You are a detective as well?" Zendejas asked, turning to Hillary.

Before she could answer, Ashley said, "This is Mr. Douglas's attorney. And also his fiancée. If we can find him, I think we can talk him into turning himself in, pleading to some lesser charges in exchange for testifying against those higher on the food chain. But we need to find him first, and that's where we're hoping you can help."

Hillary smiled at Zendejas and then sent a smoldering stare Ashley's way when the detective looked away.

The detective nodded. "We do not have a lot of extra resources or manpower, Detective Larson, and like you said, he has committed no major crime in Mexico."

"I appreciate that, Detective. All we're asking for is a BOLO. If it generates any hits, let me know, and I'll follow up on it. I wouldn't bother you at all if we had the resources down here, but we just don't."

Zendejas sat back, stroked his mustache. Then he nodded. "All right. I can put the information out. Can you give me a description of this Jackson Douglas?"

Ashley provided him the photo on her phone, then gave him all the pertinent physical descriptions. She also described his antique of a car, a 1976 Ford Granada, and its license plate. Lastly, she provided Zendejas her and Hillary's contact info, then thanked him for his time. Fifteen minutes after sitting at his cubicle, they were exiting back into the afternoon heat.

Hillary grabbed Ashley's arm. "What did I say about Jackson-like dramatics?"

"So I fudged a few facts. We got what we wanted."

"Did you get that sliding scale of morality from Jackson?"

"Come on, like you've never presented the side of a story you wanted people to hear. You're a defense attorney."

"What's that supposed to mean?"

"It means you defend the guilty people too, and you keep that particular nugget of information from the jury."

"You do sound like Jackson."

"Thank you."

"And did you really have to make me his fiancée?"

"I thought it'd sell the story," Ashley said.

Hillary exhaled a deep breath as they got back into the SUV. "You think they'll turn anything up?"

"Fifty-fifty."

"That's about what I figure. Then it's another fifty-fifty if we'll have to pay for what they find."

*　　　　*　　　　*

3:17 p.m.

CONNIE FROWNED at the air rushing in through the open windows of the taxi that had finally picked her, Maggie, and Sam up outside the café after lunch. The driver had apologized in pidgin English for the air conditioning being out, but said "the sea breeze is beautiful, no?" Beautiful, maybe, but it was doing a number on her hair.

The cab drove north on narrow streets past cheap restaurants, cheaper motels, and even cheaper housing. Connie and her third husband had spent a week doing some sort of rescue work or missions or something through his church—he'd always been a religious do-gooder sort—down in Costa Rica. It was the only time she'd seen such living conditions.

They made a sudden and sharp turn to the right. Out Connie's window, more of the same cheap buildings lined the block. On the left, a fence made of stucco-covered brick and iron bars cordoned off a large concrete parking lot. Beyond it was a stadium, made of concrete, looking like the backside of a circular staircase from their vantage point.

"Plaza Monumental de Tijuana," the cabbie said.

"Can we get in at this hour?" Sam asked from the backseat.

"Sí."

At the light, he turned left, but not onto the street. Instead, he veered onto a small paved area leading to a series of archways into the parking lot. Faded black painting above the arches spelled *"Bienvenidos."* Connie knew she should recognize the phrase, but didn't.

The driver turned under the far arch, the only one whose gate was open, and drove across the parking lot. He screeched to a stop in front of a small courtyard directly in front of the stadium. The courtyard was separated from the stadium by another brick wall, this one broken by gated turnstiles. On either side of the courtyard, ticket windows were set in small stucco and clay-shingle structures built into the wall. And just out Connie's door was a bronze statue of a matador with his cape.

Connie began digging through her purse for money to pay the driver, but Sam beat her to it. "I'll get the next one, dear," Connie said with a smile.

"Don't worry about it."

The trio got out as Maggie's phone chirped. "Hello?" she said as the cab sped away. "No, we just got here."

Connie looked up at the matador. "Criminal, isn't it?" she asked Sam as Maggie explained into the phone how it had taken forever to get a cab after lunch.

"What's that?" Sam asked.

"Bullfighting. So vulgar, killing those poor animals."

"They say it's a cultural demonstration, but I'm with you. It's just gross."

"Well," Maggie said, "they're done at the police department already. Mexican cops are putting out a BOLO for Jackson and his car."

"BOLO?" Connie asked.

"Be on the lookout."

"Shouldn't that be a BOTL?"

Sam snickered, then asked Maggie, "Are they coming here?"

"They're going to swing by the liquor store Jackson apparently frequented. Then call again." She stuck her phone into her pocket. "Should we?"

"Looks pretty deserted," Sam said.

"The host at the café said it's still bullfighting season, so there should be a ticket booth open. And there's a bookmaker just down the block too."

"When did you learn all that?"

"You really thought it took me ten minutes to go to the bathroom?"

"Now that you mention it, you were gone awhile."

Maggie smirked and led the way past the matador statue, toward a row of ticket windows.

"I thought a bolo was a tie those cowboy sorts wear," Connie said as she followed, and Sam snickered again.

Two of the three windows had "*Cerrado*" signs on them, which Connie assumed meant closed. Maggie walked up to the third, leaned on the ledge, and rapped on the window with her knuckles. She raised them to knock again when the window slid open, revealing bars behind it.

"*Hola,*" Maggie said.

"*Buenos días, señorita. ¿Sois Americanos?*"

"*Sí.* Do you speak English?"

"Yes, I speak English," he said with a wide smile, and Connie sighed with relief. "My name is Francisco. Are you ladies interested in tickets to tonight's bullfights?"

"We actually wanted to ask you about a previous fight," Maggie said.

"A previous fight?"

Maggie nodded as she leaned sideways on the ledge, enabling Connie to see her eyes. Apparently she had determined she could flirt her way to info from Francisco. Judging by the way he was grinning at her, she was right.

"I'm Maggie. This is Samantha and Connie."

"Hello," Francisco said. "What brings you all to Mexico?"

"He does," Maggie said, extending her phone to Francisco. "He attended a fight on a Saturday about a month ago."

Francisco shook his head. "Sorry, but I see thousands of faces. A lot of Americans too. They like to watch the bullfights. They like to see the blood."

Connie winced, as did Sam beside her.

"Funny you should mention blood," Maggie said. "The night he was here, there was a fight in the stands."

Francisco shrugged. "Not all that uncommon." He leaned forward, closer to Maggie. "Get fifteen to twenty thousand rowdy, screaming fans, alcohol, there will be some pushing and shoving. Sometimes even punches thrown. Our security is on top of it."

"This went beyond pushing and shoving," Maggie said. "Five or six guys were arrested, including our friend here. He was bruised and cut up, and I'm guessing he wasn't in the worst shape."

"When did you say this was?"

"Five weeks ago. September 14."

"Oh yeah, oh yeah, I remember that. Yeah, that was a big fight. I've never seen anything like that."

She showed him the phone again. "Now do you remember this man?"

"Yeah, yeah, yeah," Francisco said as if the lightbulb had gone over his head. "Yeah, now I remember him. Yeah, after the gates close, we go in to watch the fights. That one was epic. The bull took a piece out of the matador."

"A piece?" Sam asked.

"Gored him in the leg. Just a flesh wound. That bull put up quite a fight."

"Is that so?"

"*Sí, sí.* They granted him an indulgence."

"I beg your pardon?" Connie said.

"If a bull fights particularly well or displays exceptional bravery, the spectators can call for an *induito* or a pardon. If granted by the *presidente*—"

"The President was there?" Connie asked.

Francisco smiled. "The *presidente* is the presiding dignitary at the fight, not the actual president."

"And he can pardon the bull?"

"*Sí, sí.* And if so, the bull is retired to stud. Not a bad deal."

Connie frowned.

"Do you remember anything else about the fight, about him?" Maggie asked, tipping the phone with the picture of Jackson back and forth.

"No. Ah, the fight in the stands started shortly after the bull gored the matador." He shrugged. "But that is all I know."

"Is there anyone else here we can talk to?" Sam asked. "Anyone else who might have known or seen something else?"

"Juan Carlos, head of security, but he won't be here for another hour or two. And Pepe," he said with a gesture over his shoulder, "but he's new. Just started two weeks ago."

"*Gracias,*" Maggie said with a wink.

"Hey, you sure you don't want tickets to tonight's fights?"

"Maybe another time," she said, and the trio turned to leave. Instead of going back the way the cab had brought them in, they turned toward the west—toward the ocean.

"So what happened between you and Jackson?" Connie asked as she followed Maggie and Sam out of the bullring parking lot. Maggie had said something about a bookie, and he was apparently in walking distance. Connie was starting to get sick of traipsing around in the heat, especially in two-inch heels, but she wasn't going to complain. Instead, she figured some conversation would take all their minds off Jackson's predicament.

Both Maggie and Sam turned around. Then they looked at each other.

"What do you mean, what happened?" Maggie finally asked.

"Well, I used to see you both around quite a lot. Grilling on his deck, watching TV on the couch. I can see his living room from my breakfast nook, you know."

"And what, you sit there spying on his guests?"

"Well, I wouldn't call it spying. I happen to see things. Besides, I'm worried about Jackson."

"We all are," Sam said.

"I don't mean now, here," Connie said with a wave of her hand. "He's thirty-one now, getting to be an old man. It's time he settles down."

Sam looked down. Maggie smirked and turned her eyes back to the road they had turned onto. It was narrow, with ramshackle buildings on either side of it. The ocean was gray and receded into haze the same color only a lighter shade on the horizon.

"Either of you ever think about . . . you know, settling down?" Connie asked.

"You mean with Jackson?" Maggie asked.

Connie shrugged. "In general. You're both, what, mid-to-late twenties? The clock is ticking. And believe you me, it only starts ticking louder."

"There's always the snooze button," Maggie said. She lightly backhanded Sam in the arm. "What about you, Sam, you planning to settle down?" She winked.

Sam looked straight down the road for a moment. "Yeah, I've thought about it."

"Well, you'd better do more than thinking and snoozing," Connie said. She leaned forward. "If we find Jackson and he's not married to some Mexican girl, you had better make your move."

"I think she's talking to you," Maggie said.

"I'm talking to either one of you. Hillary's certainly not letting the grass grow under her feet. You should take a cue from her."

"Yeah, I'll do that," Maggie said. She pointed across the street. "We're here."

"Thank heavens," Connie said. "Let's hope it's air-conditioned."

Chapter Seven

3:41 p.m.

"WHAT KIND OF person would make a bet at *Mañoso's*?" Sam asked as the trio crossed the street.

"Why?" Connie asked. "What's *Mañoso* mean?"

"Tricky or slick," Sam answered.

"The kind of person who can't speak any Spanish," Maggie said with a grin. "Careful, don't insult a possible source."

They approached a building that looked one good ocean breeze from collapsing. It was painted half white and half blue, a single story, with a cockeyed roof that was peeling. Similarly tipsy buildings on either side may have been what was keeping it upright. There were no windows, just a screen door, allowing Bob Seger and the Silver Bullet Band to reach the sidewalk. Brown letters on a white awning over the doorway identified the place. Maggie opened the screen door with a squeak and extended it to Sam, taking the lead.

Her eyes needed a minute to adjust to the relative darkness. Then they picked out a scrawny white guy sitting in a recliner in the right corner, under a floor lamp. He had a cigarette in his mouth and a folded newspaper in his lap. He was maybe sixty, hard to tell with scruffy facial hair and a newsboy cap. He wore a bowling shirt unbuttoned over a white tank top, corduroy pants, flip-flops. The recliner was pointed at a bank of TVs on the far wall, which wasn't that far. Situated above a ticker showing various betting lines, the TVs aired a couple of soccer matches, both muted, and a baseball game that may or may not have been competing with Bob Seger. Then again, who could compete with "Against the Wind"?

Beyond the recliner was a combination bookshelf and minibar. Between the recliner and the entrance, a flimsy desk with two laptops, one open, one closed. Other than a doorway leading into even darker parts unknown and a very poor recreation of a doctor's waiting room in the left corner, the small room was empty.

Maggie cleared her throat.

"Yeah," the guy cackled, not moving. "Seven-letter word for deteriorate?"

"Um, *Mañoso's*."

He turned his head. "Cute." His eyebrows rose. "Sorry, not a margarita bar, ladies."

"We're not interested in margaritas," Maggie said.

"Speak for yourself, honey," Connie mumbled.

The guy dropped the newspaper on the desk. "You looking for a little action?"

"Looking for a little information," Maggie said.

He huffed. "I don't give out tips, sweetheart. Hard to stay in business like that, don't you think?"

"And quite the business you've got here."

"Keep 'em coming, princess. See how far you get."

Maggie reached into her pocket and pulled out a twenty-dollar bill. She flipped it onto the desk. He eyed it, then her. "I'm listening now at least."

"You *Mañoso*?"

"Yeah."

"You take action on the fights over at the bullring?"

"If the money's right, I'll take any kind of action. Why? We get our handful of Americans who come down to watch a bullfight, but you don't fit the profile, sweetie."

Maggie swallowed back the retort she wanted to say, hoping it would save her money. More flies with honey, and all that.

She held her phone to *Mañoso*. "You recognize this guy?"

"You kidding?"

"He was down here last month, looking to make a bet on a bullfight."

"You're not kidding. You think I remember every face that comes through here?"

"You mean what with all these other customers?"

"You're a real kill, sweet cheeks."

She reached for another twenty, hoping the group would chip-in to cover paying witnesses.

"You can throw all the cash you want on the table, it's not going to make me remember some random face."

"Would have been a Saturday, September 14. Don't tell me a guy like you doesn't keep records."

"His account might be in arrears," Sam said. "He was arrested that night, and maybe didn't pay up."

"Arrears? Sweetie pie, what are you talking about?"

Maggie reached out with her left hand and grabbed *Mañoso* by the collar of his shirt—it really was a bowling shirt, a pair of pins and a ball stenciled on the breast pocket—and practically lifted the old guy out of his chair. The cigarette fell from his mouth, and his eyes nearly bounced off Maggie's forehead.

"You use the word 'sweet' or some derivative of it one more time to refer to one of us, and you're going to be singing in an all soprano seniors choir, you got it, pal?"

She let go of him and he fell back, then brushed the cigarette off his pants onto the floor, stomping it out. "Okay, okay, sheesh, sw—lady."

"Name's Maggie. Now I've given you forty bucks. How about you at least try to think for a minute?"

"All right, all right. You're starting to remind me of my old lady."

"Poor thing," Connie said.

"When'd you say this fight was?"

"September 14. Five weeks ago."

"Let's see, I was at the ring that night, I think. On slow days, I head over to watch the fights, maybe take a few bets."

"You remember this guy?" Maggie said, showing him the photo again. "American, doesn't speak any Spanish, a smart-aleck."

"Might have been drunk," Connie added.

"His name's Jackson Douglas."

"Jackson?" *Mañoso* asked.

"You recognize him?" Sam asked.

"Action Jackson. Yeah, now I recognize him. He kept calling himself that."

"Action Jackson?" Connie asked.

"Yeah. He was totally wasted."

Maggie could hear Sam swallow behind her.

"Wasted?"

"Yeah. Only way to explain it."

"Explain what?"

"He was looking to take bets. On the bull."

"How's that?"

"He was putting up money that the bull would take out the matador."

Maggie looked to Connie beside her. Francisco had said something about a matador getting gored that night. And Jackson had been betting on it?

"Did he place a bet with you?" Sam asked.

"No, he didn't look like he wanted any formal action. More like challenging people in his section to take his bet." *Mañoso* laughed. "Yeah, now I remember him, of course. The fool was yelling for the bull, cheering him on. Made some folks pretty mad."

"Yeah," Maggie said, "we heard he got arrested for being drunk and disorderly, got in a fight."

"I didn't see that. I didn't like my chances in that crowd, so I went to find some other customers."

"You see anything else, notice anything else?"

"Nope, afraid not. I moved on and that was it. Forgot about him till you said his name a moment ago."

"Thanks," Maggie said.

"Yeah, sure. Worth another twenty, maybe?"

"Forget it, sweet cheeks," she said.

"Yeah, yeah." He sat back down, lifting his paper off the desk.

"You got any letters?" Maggie asked before turning to go.

"What?"

"Seven-letter word for deteriorate."

He looked down. "Third one's a C."

Maggie nodded, gesturing for Connie and Sam to leave. She followed them, pausing in the open doorway. "Decline."

She saw the old man wink, then heard a "Thanks, sweet thing," as she let the screen door slam.

*　　　　　*　　　　　*

3:48 p.m.

"ARE YOU a Christian, Hillary?" Ashley asked out of the blue as they drove back west across Tijuana. She leaned an elbow on the doorframe, head tilted, twirling loose strands of hair. Hillary had been staring out the window somberly most of the ride, and now looked slowly toward Ashley.

"Yes."

"My parents were Catholic, but I couldn't tell you more than the basics. The reason I ask," she said, raising her head, "is that Jackson was a Christian too."

"Was?"

Ashley turned. "I meant was as in when I knew him, talked to him, interacted with him frequently."

Hillary nodded.

"My question is, where does getting drunk fall on the Christian scale? That's taboo, right?"

"Yeah. The Bible's pretty clear drunkenness is a sin."

"What about just drinking?"

Hillary licked her lips. "That would depend on who you ask. Some Christians don't have any problem drinking. Some see it as sin. Some used to struggle with drinking and so don't touch alcohol, regardless of its sinfulness or lack thereof."

"What's your take?"

"I think the Bible says drunkenness is a sin, not drinking."

"What did Jackson think?"

"Well, that was kind of odd. Because Jackson would break about every rule in the book, but he was a stickler on not touching alcohol."

"Ever?"

"Not that I knew. He railed against it like a traveling revival preacher."

Ashley returned her hand to her hair, fluffing it until she dropped her hand almost in frustration. "So how does he get to be a sloppy drunk getting arrested at a bullfight?"

"The same way he got to be a tree-burning stoner one Friday night."

"Yeah, but . . . that's not Jackson."

"What's not?"

"Throwing his convictions away on a whim."

Hillary huffed. "What convictions?"

"You don't think Jackson had convictions?"

"No, he has convictions. They just aren't always the strongest."

"What do you mean?"

"I mean, he can justify almost anything for his cause, the end justifying the means, a sliding scale of morality that let him date multiple women at once and still make a pass at a skirt and a reasonable wig."

"You really don't think much of him, do you?"

"I've tried," Hillary said at last. "But every time I get close, he does something again to . . . Like this. He's not only running away from life's problems, but also drowning his sorrows in liquor, getting into trouble, getting arrested again. Once is an outlier, two is a—"

"Cry for help?"

Hillary said nothing.

"And you don't think there's a good explanation for it all?"

"What, that he's working undercover to rescue a cute reporter from the cartels or trying to find a kittenish, barely-legal runaway?"

"I just mean, we're all questioning how what we're finding could be true, looking for the good. You seem to have no trouble believing the worst."

"Past experience," Hillary said, then pointed to a streetlight. "You want to turn up here."

Ashley did, and rolled to the curb in front of *Brisa Licores* a block later. It was a hole in the wall, bar-lined windows on either side of double glass doors filled with bottles of liquor and painted with deals and discounts. "How do you want to play this?" Ashley asked.

"Straight."

"Lead the way."

They got out and walked to the front door, earning a whistle from a pair of guys passing by on the sidewalk. Hillary sent them a glare that threatened to leave holes in their skulls.

A bell tinkled above the door as they entered. *Brisa Licores* was twice as deep as wide, comprising several aisles, all stacked from top to bottom with various alcoholic beverages. Wine to tequila, bourbon to beer. A U-shaped counter with an old-fashioned cash register was in the middle, backed by a wall with boxes of cigarettes stacked against it. Two huge mirrors hung over either "corner" of the U, enabling the clerk to see into the back of the store. It appeared empty, and Ashley followed Hillary to the counter.

"Hola, señoritas," the clerk said. He had a balding head, but for patches above the ears, and a thick mustache. He wore a black T-shirt with Bob Marley smoking a joint on the front, but it was the only Rastafarian influence in the shop. *"¿Qué puedo hacer por ustedes?"* he asked.

"¿Habla Inglés?"

"Sí, sí, I speak English. Some, at least. I am Hector."

"Hillary. Ashley."

"Ah, pleased to meet you, *señoritas.*"

"We're looking for a friend of ours," Hillary said, doing a pretty good job not choking on the word "friend." The five women had swapped a few pictures of Jackson, so they all had one on their phone, and Hillary showed it to Hector. "We were told he frequented your store, about a month ago."

"Sí, sí, I recognize him. *Sí,* he came in a few times. Has it been a month already?"

"Do you know what he purchased?" Hillary asked.

"Sí, sí, it's why I remember him, other than for the fact not many *Americanos* come into my store."

Hillary waited, the impatience practically coming out of her pores.

"He bought a couple bottles of cheap tequila—and several cases of cheap beer. Always the cheapest."

Hillary emitted a soft huff.

"Do you remember how many times he came in?" Ashley asked.

"*Sí, sí.* Two, maybe three, while I was here. I am here most of the time."

"And he purchased the same thing each time?" Hillary asked.

"No, no. The first time just a couple bottles of tequila and a six-pack. The next time, a couple cases, maybe another bottle. I don't remember too much."

Hillary sighed and reached into her purse for a ten-dollar bill. "Would this help you remember?"

"No, no, *señorita*. I am not trying to take your money. I just don't remember."

"Anything else you do remember?" Ashley asked.

"No. Well, maybe. The second time, he looked as if he had been in a fight." Hector gestured to his head. "Cuts, bruises."

"Thank you," Hillary said, returning the money to her purse.

Ashley smiled at Hector, thanked him as well, and followed Hillary outside. "Lucky," she said.

"How's that?" Hillary asked.

"Saved your ten bucks."

"I'm sorry, do I not bribe informants properly for you?"

"He's not an informant. And I wanted to cut you off at the pass," Ashley said as she circled the front of the Rogue, "because I'm sure you're about to make a crack about how cheap Jackson was."

They got in.

"Look," Hillary said, "I told you all when you begged me to come along, Jackson and I aren't pals. We don't exactly think the world of each other."

"Yeah, I get that," Ashely said, turning the ignition. "But it's like every word out of your mouth is running him down." She turned Hillary's way. "If I didn't know better, I'd think you were compensating."

"Compensating?"

"You know, the old *Hamlet* line, about the lady protesting too much."

Ashley's phone rang before Hillary could reply, and she fished it out of the center console. "Detective Larson."

"Wow, formal," Maggie said.

"Sorry, habit."

"Where are you?"

"Just leaving the liquor store."

"Wanna swing by and pick us up?"

"At the bullring?"

"Just west of it, outside a place called *Mañoso's*."

"Chips and salsa?"

"Bookie."

"Ah. We'll be there as soon as possible."

"Thanks."

Ashley ended the call, and she and Hillary drove to pick up Connie, Maggie, and Sam without another word.

Chapter Eight

5:52 p.m.

"THE HOTEL CALIFORNIA?" Maggie asked.

"What's wrong with that?" Ashley asked as she turned the Rogue into the parking lot of a two-story motel a few blocks inland. The Rogue rumbled across the broken pavement connecting the street to the parking lot in front of an L-shaped burnt orange—almost the same color as the Rogue—building. Sam and Ashley had selected the hotel based on its rates, online photos and reviews, and its location on a strip of *Paseo Playas de Tijuana* that was home to several restaurants and hotels and appeared reasonably tourist friendly.

"I know it's not the nicest place, and a little kitschy, but it seemed like a reasonable option," Sam said.

"I'm not disputing that. I'm just talking about the name."

"What's wrong with the name?" Ashley asked. "This is Baja California, isn't it?"

Maggie grinned.

"What?"

"The Hotel California?"

She parked and looked back at Maggie, a blank expression on her face. "Yeah?"

"The song by the Eagles."

"Who?"

"Oh my goodness," Connie muttered.

"How old are you again?" Maggie asked.

Ashley turned off the engine. "Not as old as you, apparently."

"Touché," Maggie said with a wink.

"Are we staying?" Connie asked.

"We're staying," Maggie said, opening her door. The five got out. They had spent the latter part of the afternoon fruitlessly. Maggie and Hillary had hung around *Plaza Monumental de Tijuana*, waiting to talk to Juan Carlos, the head of security. First, they had checked with several local hotels to see if Jackson happened to have checked in. Sam, Ashley, and Connie had driven to several hotels near *El Hotel Pacífico* under the same auspices, figuring Jackson may not have wanted to wander too far from his current haunts—and his current liquor store. Neither group had located him, and Juan Carlos had been handling another matter at the time of the fight on the fourteenth, and could do little but corroborate what was in the police report.

Speaking of the police, Ashley had tracked down a phone number and address for Officer Franco, one of the two arresting officers, the one who hadn't been to work in three days, according to Officer Peña. No one had answered the phone, and he lived across town, so they had ruled out driving to his house. Current odds were that he had been snuffed out by the cartels or disappeared after taking a bribe.

While Connie had been using the restroom at the last hotel they checked, Sam and Ashley had scouted motels on their phones and settled on the Hotel California. Now that Maggie mentioned it, the name did sound familiar, but Sam couldn't place it. And she'd heard of the Eagles, but never listened to them.

"How many rooms?" Maggie asked.

"Two. A pair of queens and a pair of doubles with a pull-out."

"I can take the pull-out," Sam volunteered.

"I'll flip you for it," Maggie said. "Else a double."

"Well, I'd prefer not a pull-out," Connie said, "but I certainly don't need a queen bed all myself."

"Three of us, two of you?" Maggie asked, looking at Ashley and Hillary.

"Fine," Hillary said. Ashley shrugged, and it was settled. They checked in, then discussed dinner. They voted unanimously to get carry-out, and Connie—the gourmet—volunteered to go. There were several places in walking distance, and Hillary opted to go with her, it seemed to blow off steam. She'd been in a bad mood most of the afternoon, Sam thought.

The rooms were simple and threadbare, but reasonably clean. The doors reached the floors, and there weren't any bugs or lizards visible. The water was likely undrinkable, but Ashley had brought along two packages of bottled water. They split one in each room, then Connie and Hillary set off in search of something that would suit everyone's palette, and Ashley retreated to her room to "check in on some things." Maggie had to "use the head," so Sam wandered out onto the balcony. Technically, it was just an external corridor, connecting all the rooms on the second floor of the motel. Theirs was facing west, across the parking lot, the street, several blocks of the city, and a low-hanging, haze-obscured orange sun. The breeze was out of the south, warm and sultry, a perfect complement to Sam's current mood.

She didn't hear Maggie until she leaned on the railing beside her. She had changed into a black ribbed tank top and piled her hair behind her head. Her appearance seemed to epitomize to Sam how at ease Maggie was, like nothing threw her. Comfortable in her own skin, just like Jackson.

"In an odd way, it's kind of beautiful," Maggie said after a minute or two.

"What's that?"

"This." She nodded toward the sunset. "It's authentic, no pretenses."

"I guess."

"And a sunset's a sunset."

Sam nodded.

Maggie turned. "You all right?"

Sam looked at her, unable to see through gold-rimmed aviator sunglasses to Maggie's eyes. Slowly, she shook her head. "No. Everything we're hearing about Jackson . . . it goes against everything I've ever known about him, and yet . . ."

"It doesn't," Maggie said.

"Yeah."

"People are complex. Not all good or all bad. And we want to think they are, but it's not true."

"No." Sam sighed. "You know last time, people kept telling me Jackson could take care of himself. It's what he always said, in his own way. 'Don't worry, I'll be fine.' And I started to believe it, even with everything that happened to him, even after March. But what scares me, Maggie, is what if he doesn't want to take care of himself? What if it's like you said earlier, that he's lost the will to live?"

Maggie didn't answer, and Sam leaned harder on the railing. She tried to take solace in the gentleness of the breeze as it lifted hair off her shoulders or the brilliance of the sunset. Neither provided any.

"It's like Ashley said. That's why we're here."

Sam turned to Maggie. "What if we aren't enough? We got nowhere today."

"Maybe. And I still have faith in Jack. He might bottom out, but . . . after everything he's been through, he's always gotten back up. Always kept going. He'll do it again."

"I hope you're right."

A distant siren sounded, grew closer, then faded. Sirens meant crime and injury and danger, not what Sam needed at the moment.

"Can I ask you something?" Maggie said, looking at Sam with a cockeyed expression.

"Yeah."

"You don't have to answer if you don't want, but I feel like we're sort of dancing around this thing here. What exactly was your relationship with Jackson?"

Sam swallowed.

"You were his nurse after he got shot, you showed up at the hospital after the whole Russian thing. You're on Ashley's rolodex now." She shrugged. "I'm not jealous. Just curious."

Sam nodded. "Thing is, we never really defined what it was. I wasn't his girlfriend or anything, but we . . . I'd guess you say we dated. Dinner and a movie, tennis and iced tea on his deck, that sort of thing."

"Dodger games, pinball and cheeseburgers, *Magnum* reruns," Maggie said. "And nothing defined."

Sam's heart was pounding, and she didn't know why. She wasn't jealous of Maggie either, at least she didn't think so.

"He said you were a friend from church, after he got shot and I caught you—well, not caught—patching him up."

"He said you were a client."

Maggie grinned. "I sort of was."

"So he was dating both of us," Sam said.

"Looks that way," Maggie said, taking off her sunglasses.

"I can't believe it."

"Yeah, well, I sort of can."

"I wonder . . ."

Maggie let her think. She did it out loud. "He never seemed interested in anything more. And I never really did either. You think that was it?"

"Jack and I had a couple conversations about our 'relationship,'" Maggie said with air quotes. "He basically said there was no real potential for us since I didn't share his faith."

"I'm sure he said that very delicately," Sam said.

"Oh, of course." Maggie grinned. "After I got saved, I said that wasn't an issue anymore, and we could pursue something. He said we should give it a little while."

"You think that was because of me?" Sam asked.

"I think you're one of the reasons he and I never got serious, and I think I'm one of the reasons you and he never did. Truth be told, I never wanted anything serious. Not sure I do now."

"You mean with Jackson?"

"With anybody," Maggie said with a shrug. "I'm kind of a free spirit, you know? I'm not sure I'm ready for wife and mother territory. Or for that matter, to be a one-man woman."

Sam couldn't help letting her eyebrows rise.

"I don't mean that the way it sounds. But even if he'd have been up for it, I wasn't ready to commit to just Jackson. I clearly wasn't ready to commit to just Russell. I like . . . freelancing."

Sam nodded.

"So what happened with you and Jack? You said you hadn't seen him much."

"I was ready," Sam said. "I thought. And I couldn't see the life I wanted—a wife and mother, a home with a picket fence," she said with a thin smile. "I couldn't see that with Jackson and his 'baddy'-busting lifestyle. Then I met Jeff."

"Jeff know you're down here chasing an old not-boyfriend?"

Sam looked directly at her, into her gray-blue eyes. "We broke up."

"I'm sorry."

"I don't know, I . . . Things were moving along fast, and I thought I was ready, but I don't think I was. I don't know."

"It's funny," Maggie said. "Here we sit ragging on Jack, and maybe we're the ones who can't commit."

"Yeah," Sam said softly.

Maggie leaned into her, bumping her arm. "Just so you know, there's no bad blood from my side."

"Bad blood?"

"Between us. Because we sort of shared Jackson."

"Oh, right. Yeah, me either."

"Although if we find him, we should play it up that there is, see if we can make him squirm. He does deserve that much, at least."

"*If* we find him?"

"When we find him," Maggie said.

Sam nodded.

A few minutes passed.

"Can I ask you something else?" Maggie asked.

"Sure."

"You still have a thing for Jackson?"

Sam looked down, then turned her head to Maggie. "I don't know."

"*When* we find him, you should figure that out. For his sake and yours."

Sam nodded again as the sun dipped into the haze over the ocean and darkness began to fall over Mexico.

*   *   *

6:20 p.m.

"SO WHAT do we do now?" Sam asked as the five women sat around on the pull-out sofa, beds, and floor of the room she shared with Connie and Maggie. Connie and Hillary had found an American Chinese carry-out restaurant in the heart of Mexico, found its menu suitable, and ordered plenty of General Tso's chicken, sweet and sour pork, fried rice, and vegetables. It hadn't been the sort of gourmet meal Connie had envisioned when planning a trip south of the border, but for what it was, it wasn't bad.

"Hope Tijuana PD's BOLO gets a hit," Maggie said before shoveling in some sweet and sour pork.

"And if it doesn't? Do we sit around and wait or is there more we can do?"

There had been a small debate about whether or not the group wanted to spend the night in Mexico or return to the U.S. They weren't ready to give up, and decided to avoid a couple more border crossings and extra travel—and stay potentially close to Jackson.

"There's more," Ashley said. "We can track down Officer Franco, check out more hotels—"

"Digging for a needle in a haystack," Hillary said.

"If the ro—"

"I know, I know, if the roles were reversed, Jackson would move heaven and earth, stop the sun in its orbit, save the universe."

"You forgetting what happened in Nevada?" Maggie asked from where she sat cross-legged on the floor.

"No, I am not forgetting," Hillary said before taking a bite of veggies.

"Seriously, what did he do to you, anyhow?" Ashley asked.

Hillary set down her takeout box on the window sill. "I'm just tired of everybody talking about Jackson as if he's a saint. Yes, he saved my life. Yes, I owe him. Yes, I saw a different side of him that week. But the preponderance of evidence suggests Jackson Douglas is a life-long slacker, a skirt-chasing deadbeat, and he's done exactly what everyone has been telling us today—he ran away to Mexico to drink himself sloppy, start trouble, and flirt with random hotel guests and hookers."

Connie caught glares directed at Hillary from Ashley and Maggie as she reached for the General Tso's chicken. For a few minutes, the group ate in silence.

"Let's review what we know," Ashley said finally. "Without adding any of our own opinions."

Hillary said nothing.

"We know he came to Mexico a little over a month ago," Sam said. "We know he sent a postcard to Reggie about how hot the girls were here."

Hillary huffed softly.

"He checked into *El Hotel Pacífico* on the tenth," Maggie said, chopsticking some pork, "and was kicked out on the eighteenth."

"While there, he drank a lot of alcohol," Connie said.

"No," Sam said. "We know he purchased a lot of alcohol."

"You don't think he drank it?"

"Did the bartender tell you he saw Jackson drinking it?"

Connie looked at Maggie, then Ashley.

"I don't think so, but we didn't ask," Ashley said. "We assumed," she added with a look of self-condemnation.

"Why would he buy it if he wasn't going to drink it?" Connie asked.

"Manny did say he was buying the women all the booze they could drink," Maggie said.

"And everyone has told us he seemed drunk—Officer Peña, Gloria, *Mañoso*," Sam said. "But nobody actually saw him drinking or checked his blood alcohol level or anything."

"It seems like a slam dunk," Ashley said, "but I'll grant your point."

"You think he was faking?" Hillary asked.

Sam shrugged.

"Why would he fake being drunk?"

"I don't know. But she said review what we *know*," Sam said with a nod at Ashley.

She swallowed. "I did."

"And we don't *know* Jackson drank the alcohol."

"Well, then we don't *know* he was the one who sent the postcard to Reggie, do we? And if Jackson didn't drink the alcohol, we need a reason for his behavior. Believe me, 'he might not have done it' isn't a viable defense unless you can at the very least suggest a possible alternative."

"Even if you have a strong character witness?" Sam asked.

"Do you?"

"Yes. I know what you said about Jackson before, but I'd vouch for his character any day. And before I'm going to believe that he was drunk or hired a prostitute, I'm going to need rock-solid proof."

"That's fair," Ashley said. "What else do we *know*?"

"He got into a fight at a bullfight," Maggie said. "And was cheering for the bull."

"Is that relevant?" Connie asked. "I mean, this whole bullfighting thing seems out of character for Jackson."

"This whole Mexico thing does."

"True. But it's such an oddity, isn't it?"

"Not if he was looking to cause trouble," Ashley said. "Go to a public place, set yourself against the majority of the people there, be belligerent."

"Why would he want to cause trouble?" Sam asked.

Ashley shrugged.

"He's been depressed lately," Connie added. "So you all claim, at least. And he didn't seem himself to me, either."

"He's ignoring his friends," Ashley said.

"Not listening to Reggie," Maggie added.

"Who said he'd been drinking, didn't he?" Hillary asked.

Sam looked down.

"Okay," Ashley said, "fair summary? Jack's been even more depressed than typical, went to Mexico to 'get away,' lounged around at the hotel for a while, bought—and thus reasonably likely drank—a lot of alcohol, was at the least an instigator of a fight at a bullfight that led to him getting arrested, and was wild and loud enough to get kicked out of his hotel."

Connie saw three heads nod, and did as well.

"So where does that leave us? What is he doing here?"

"Nothing good," Connie said, digging into her takeout box.

"Are we missing a possibility?" Maggie asked.

"What's that?"

"He's working a case."

"Reggie said he wasn't," Sam said.

"Maybe he didn't tell Reggie."

"His best friend?" Ashley asked.

"Who he's sort of on the outs with."

Ashley looked around.

"You're saying he's trying to convince everyone he's down here playing the leering lush, and he's actually working a case somewhere—here or elsewhere?" Hillary asked.

"Just asking if it's possible."

"Possible, I suppose," Ashley said. "But if that's the case, we're not going to find him. And probably shouldn't."

Sam shook her head. "After what happened in March, I can't believe he'd keep Reggie out of the loop, even if they were going through a rough patch."

"Yeah, probably not. Just spit-balling."

Ashley sighed, for the group it seemed. "Until we find out something more, I guess we really don't *know* anything."

Chapter Nine

INCESSANT KNOCKING GREW louder and louder as Maggie approached the hotel door. She tousled her drying hair and muttered an "I'm coming," as she reached for the doorknob.

Jackson stood on the balcony, dressed in a swimsuit with a towel around his neck. He was dripping wet, smirking like a dork. There was a woman on each arm, both Latina. The one on his right was dressed in a slinky, high-cut dress with sequins all over it. She had tons of makeup, pouty lips, and eyes that challenged Maggie even as the woman leaned further into Jackson, whose right hand was tight around her waist.

His left hand held two longneck bottles of Coors as it was draped over the shoulders of a woman in a bikini. She kissed his cheek, then took the brand new Los Angeles Dodgers baseball cap from his head and placed it over her long, black hair. Then she settled into his shoulder, her look at Maggie practically defiant.

"Hey, Mags, how's it going?" Jackson asked.

She was speechless.

"We're gonna go hit up the Spanish equivalent of B-Dubs for all-you-can-eat wings and beer." He winked his eyebrows. "You in?"

Maggie tried to reply, to ask a dozen questions, but before she could, Ashley and Hillary moved in from her right and left respectively. Ashley slapped a pair of handcuffs on the girl in the bikini, pulling her out from under Jackson's arm, causing the Dodgers hat to fall off and him to drop one of the bottles of Coors on top of it. At the same time, Hillary began lecturing the woman in the slinky dress about the ills of prostitution. They disappeared, leaving just Jackson in front of Maggie.

"Well," he said, leaning his free hand on the doorpost. "What say you and I get out of here, go grab some Finn-Skins maybe?"

Before she could answer again, Sam pushed past her onto the balcony. She was dressed in hospital scrubs, and first whacked Jackson on the shoulder with a clipboard, then lassoed him with her stethoscope and pulled him away. He gave Maggie a fleeting wink and was gone.

Maggie's eyes snapped open, looking at inconsistent popcorn texture on the ceiling. The room was poorly lit and quiet. The door was closed. Water quit running in the bathroom. Maggie sat up, throwing off the sheet she'd been sleeping under and swinging her legs over the side of her double bed. The other—Connie's—was empty. The pullout was folded back into a sofa, sheets folded under a pillow on one arm.

Maggie ran her hands over her face and through her hair, then got up to get a bottle of water. She drank a quarter of it, and splashed another quarter on her face and neck. She sat back on the edge of the bed with a creak. She wanted to blame the dream on the Chinese food, but knew she couldn't.

After a minute, she stood and then, to see what kind of day it was and to shake the image that Jackson would be standing there with two "friends," she opened the door.

It was raining, the sky a dull gray canvas. Thunder or a truck rumbled in the distance, and she closed the door. As she did, Ashley stepped out of the bathroom.

"Hey, you're up."

"I'm up," Maggie said.

"You okay?"

"Yeah, no I'm fine."

"Connie and Sam went to get breakfast, and they let me shower here. My roommate's primping like she's got closing arguments today."

Maggie nodded. She turned over her shoulder, having a little trouble getting her brain in gear this morning. "They went in the rain."

Ashley waved. "I let them take the Rogue." She gestured at the bathroom. "You want in? I'm done."

"Sure, thanks."

Maggie took a little extra time in the shower, waking fully up and wondering if the dream had meant anything. Not in the Joseph and the cupbearer sort of way, but the way she'd heard the brain processed events of the day and replayed them in its dreams. Jackson flaunting a couple of floozies on his arm, then being taken away by Sam. Did that have anything to do with what they'd learned yesterday or with Maggie and Sam's talk about sort-of-dating Jackson? More to the point, did it suggest Maggie wasn't content being a "freelancer" and letting the idea of her and Jackson go? Then again, she'd once dreamed she'd stalked a columnist from her old employer, the *Los Angeles Times*, and his family, trying to steal him away so they could retire in Napa together. And she hadn't held the least amount of romantic feelings for the columnist. She'd chalked that up to the absurd nature of dreams, and as she dressed in clean jeans, another tank top, and a gray-and-black checked shirt she did the same with her dream of Jackson.

The room was empty when she came out of the bathroom, so she set some coffee brewing—The Hotel California at least had a coffee pot— and turned on the TV. She had no interest watching anything *en Español*, but figured she might at least catch a radar on a weather forecast. The last thing the group needed to do was spend a day traipsing around after clues in the rain.

Connie and Sam returned as the weather girl for one of the local stations promised the rain would move out by midday. She didn't back up that prediction with radar. Hillary—who was indeed spiffed up—was right behind Connie and Sam, who brought breakfast burritos and fresh fruit to go with leftover sticky buns and muffins. Ashley arrived a minute later, as they were divvying up the food.

"I just got off the phone with Detective Zendejas," she said.

All four perked up.

"Jackson's Granada was found in the parking lot of a hotel in Ensenada."

"Where is Ensenada?" Connie asked.

"About fifty miles south of here," Ashley said.

"Did they find Jackson?" Sam asked.

"He said a routine state police patrol spotted the plate from the BOLO, called it in, and that was it."

"They didn't check it out?"

"Weren't asked to," Ashley said. "And I don't think the cops around here do more than they're asked to."

Connie harrumphed.

"That's something, at least," Maggie said.

"Should we call the hotel?"

"I'd rather go in person," Ashley said.

"Afraid you'll spook him?" Hillary asked.

"Sort of, actually. I'd rather knock on his door instead of giving some hotel clerk an hour or two to warn him."

"Warn him?" Sam asked. "You seriously think he might be trying to run from us?"

"Not from us, but from anyone looking for him. I don't know. I just want to be careful."

"Then let's eat and get moving," Connie said.

Maybe Maggie's dream had been something of a vision, a premonition. Swimsuits and slinky sidekicks aside, maybe she'd be the one knocking on Jackson's door with a smart-aleck "hey there," before the day was done.

*   *   *

10:36 a.m.

HILLARY SAT in the backseat of the Rogue, passenger side, as the group drove south. The highway followed the coast, and even with the rain, the scenery was nice. The fact that Jackson's car had been spotted was a positive sign, Hillary had to conclude. And yet, the deeper they penetrated into Mexico in search of him, the worse she felt.

Part of that was because of the recriminations she'd received for her criticism of Jackson. But, for all he had done for her in Nevada and for the slight uptick in their relations since, his alleged current behavior—and it was beyond alleged in her book—conspired with everything she had known about him for years to color her perspective. And yet, here she was.

Jackson's Granada had been spotted in the parking lot of *El Saguaro*, a cheap motel offering daily, weekly, or monthly rates—per TripAdvisor.com—in a touristy section of Ensenada. The city of half a million was built in the valley around the horseshoe-shaped All Saints Bay. Jackson's hotel, like most of the rest in the city, was within a few blocks of the man-made harbor that accommodated the Port of Ensenada, including cruise ship docks, a naval base, a couple of marinas, government offices, and city parks. For Mexico, it wasn't a bad part of town. Certainly an improvement from *El Hotel Pacífico*.

With Maggie navigating, Ashley found her way off the highway, onto a side street lined with cheap souvenir shops, bars and cantinas, and motels. *El Saguaro* was painted bright yellow with a green, three-dimensional cactus extending from the wall protecting an open stairway—a wall that also served as the "front" of the building. The office was directly beside it, opposite a small, cramped parking lot. The hotel was three stories tall, shaped like a U around the parking lot, with exterior corridors like at The Hotel California. Connected to the office and facing the street was *El Saguaro Café*. A scattering of palm trees backed the office and café, suggesting a pool area lay beyond them. As Ashley turned into the parking lot, Hillary spied a walkway behind the stairs, leading from the parking lot to a pool. If it had a minibar, Jackson may never have to leave.

"There it is," Sam said, pointing to the far corner of the lot. Glinting in filtered sun that was chasing away the rain was the red paint of Jackson's Granada. Ashley parked as close to it as she could, two spots away, and the five women got out.

The air was cool compared to the day before, but the lack of breeze and filtered sun beating down on faded blacktop were heating it quickly. Hillary stretched and walked around the back of the Rogue. "Check at the office?" she asked Ashley.

"Hmm? Yeah," she said, having stooped to peer into the Granada's passenger window. Maggie had wandered around to the driver's side.

NATHAN BIRR

"See anything?" Sam asked.

"Take-out wrappers, coffee cups," Ashley said.

Maggie tried the door. "Locked," she said.

"Did he keep a spare key somewhere?" Sam asked. "You know, under the wheel well or something?"

None of them knew. Hillary kept her eyes roving the doors and windows of the various rooms at *El Saguaro* in case a shaggy, unshaven face peeked out. She saw nothing.

"Let's check at the front desk," Ashley finally said. "See if he's here."

They crossed the parking lot. Across the street was a small motel, a tattoo parlor, a pharmacy, and a T-shirt shop, with a cantina on the corner. Pedestrians lined the sidewalks, and Latino hip-hop blared out of one of the shops. The smells from the cantina—or maybe *El Saguaro Café*—wafted down the street, and weren't terrible.

The office was accessible from the corner where the sidewalk met the parking lot. Sam held the door for the others, and they entered a room as bright as the exterior of the hotel, only in lime green. A wall split the office in two but for a large mission-style arch carved out of it, underneath which was a long counter paneled in bright, garish subway tiles. Mounted on the wall behind the desk was a cubby containing slots for mail, and beneath it, a pegboard half full of numbered keys. The office was empty, on both sides of the desk, and Hillary could just see an open door on the other side, leading out toward a patio. Their side had two uncomfortable looking chairs, a couple of potted plants, and a rack of brochures. That and a door to the café.

Connie stepped forward and dinged a bell on the counter. A few seconds later, a man in slacks and a short-sleeved button-down shirt entered from the patio. *"Buenos días. Lo siento por el retraso. ¿Como puedo ayudarles?"*

It came out in a torrent, followed by a toothy smile. He was young, maybe awestruck by all his guests. At any rate, Ashley went through the routine of finding out if he spoke English, and he did. He repeated his question. "How can I help you?"

"We're looking for a guest of yours," Ashley said. "His name is Jackson Douglas."

"Douglas, Douglas, Douglas," he said, looking at something under the counter. "Ah, *Señor* Douglas. Yes." He frowned.

"What is it?" Ashley asked.

"He is due to check out this morning. And . . ." He consulted a watch. "Within just a few minutes, in fact."

"Can you tell us which room he's in?" Ashley asked.

"Two-fourteen," the man said. "Right across the way."

"Thank you."

They exited the office and stood facing the U-shaped hotel. Room 214 was in the corner, above the Granada.

"How do we play this?" Connie asked.

"Nothing to play," Hillary said. "We go knock on the door."

"What if he squirts?" Maggie asked.

"Trip him," Ashley said, taking the lead again. They climbed the stairs, behind the wall with the cactus, and walked around the U to room 214. Ashley got there first, and without hesitation, banged her fist on the door. Nobody answered.

Hillary tried looking in the window, but the curtains were drawn tight.

Ashley knocked again, hard enough that the door rattled. Still no answer. She turned to the group. "Out to lunch?"

"Asleep," Maggie said.

"Drunk," Hillary said.

"Chasing pretty *señoritas*," Connie said with a shrug.

"He'd kick the door down right now," Ashley said.

"And then tell the manager he was chasing a cartel boss," Maggie said.

"Won't be necessary," Hillary said, nodding behind her. The man from the front desk was headed their way.

"Excuse me, ladies," he said. "It is after eleven o'clock—checkout time."

"He's not answering," Ashley said.

"I will open the door for you. *Señor* Douglas paid for one month in advance, so his bill is up to date."

"So you can evict him?" Maggie asked.

The man nodded without a smile. Then he stepped forward and turned the key in the lock. As he did, the smells of a blend of expired food and beer rushed out. Hillary winced, but followed the man into the room. It was dark, and he flipped on a light switch, revealing a Spartan room—one bed, a dresser with a TV, an end chair and small table, a bathroom in the back. It was, in short, a pigsty. Dozens of food containers, mostly empty, were strewn everywhere. So were empty cans of beer. Dirty clothes—everything from shirts to socks—spilled out of a duffel bag on the end chair, and were littered around the room. The only saving grace was there wasn't a brassiere hanging over the TV or lamp on the nightstand.

Ashley summarized for everyone with a sigh. "Crap."

Chapter Ten

11:04 a.m.

"I'LL CHECK THE bathroom," Maggie said hesitantly, then stepped on the rare places where threadbare carpet was visible.

"When was the last time you saw him?" Ashley asked the manager, who stood beside her, mouth agape.

"I honestly don't know. I don't even remember him checking in."

She showed him her phone.

He shook his head. "Not familiar, sorry. But it has been a month."

"What about maids?"

"We only clean the rooms between guests, so none of them would have been in his room."

"You have a pool bar, anything like that?"

"No, just a pool. He may have eaten at the café, but I don't know."

"All his stuff's here," Maggie said, coming back from the bathroom. "It's a mess too."

"This isn't like him," Sam said.

"Well, he's not exactly Martha Stewart," Connie said.

"No, but this?"

"He was depressed, didn't care anymore . . ." Hillary said.

"His car's still here," Ashley said. "That means he didn't go far."

"Or it means he has a friend giving him a ride, took a taxi, is sitting in jail."

Ashley sighed.

"What do we do?" Connie asked.

"If we weren't here, what would you do?" Maggie asked the manager.

"I'm afraid *Señor* Douglas only paid through last night, so we would clean out his room."

"We'll pack his stuff up," Sam said.

"And do what with it?" Hillary asked.

"I don't know. Wait for him to come back?"

"You volunteering? To pack, I mean."

"I will," Sam said.

"I'm going to have a look around the grounds," Ashley said.

"I'll check the café," Hillary said.

"Guess I'll help you pack stuff up," Maggie said.

The group split, and Ashley walked down to the pool, which was a blocky, rust-stained hole in the concrete. The patio around it was cracked. Half the chairs were in a state of disrepair, and two of the three umbrellas over tables in one corner were torn and broken. At least the palm trees against a sky now showing patches of blue were lovely.

The back end of the patio opened to an alley, or would have if not for an eight-foot-tall iron fence, painted yellow and chipping badly. Across the aisle was the backside of a nondescript building on the next street. Ashley crossed the parking lot to the far side of the hotel, finding it was also bordered by an alley. Another hotel was next down the street.

She returned to the second floor, where Connie was camped outside Jackson's door. "I just can't believe this," Connie said. "What a mess."

Hillary had since returned as well, reporting that Jackson was not dining at *El Saguaro Café*. Maggie and Sam had packed most of Jackson's things into his bag, which Maggie now held as if it contained biotoxins. After a few minutes, the group decided to split up again. Connie, Hillary, and Sam would canvas the neighborhood—see if Jackson had visited some of the nearby shops or eateries. They would also keep an eye on the Granada and his room, in case he returned.

Ashley and Maggie, meanwhile, set out for the *Policia Estatal*—or the State Police—in southern Ensenada. Ashley figured they would have a wider net, a better chance of finding any crimes Jackson had committed. Plus it had been a state police patrol that had spotted the Granada.

"I'm surprised Hillary didn't want to go along again," Maggie said after directing Ashley onto the highway that would take them most of the way across town. "She is the legal eagle."

"I don't think she's real enthralled with me."

"Oh?"

"Slight disagreement over my methods at procuring information, and we have differing views about the quality of Jackson's character, or lack thereof."

Maggie nodded.

"Between you and me, I'm wondering if we made a mistake bringing her."

Maggie shrugged. "She may come in useful yet."

"To get Jackson out of trouble with the authorities, for instance?"

"For instance."

"Let's hope it doesn't come to that."

They coasted to a stop at a light. At least traffic lights meant the same thing in Mexico. Ashley was getting sick of translating and conjugating and trying to figure out the sex of words before she used them.

"On another between you and me note," Maggie said, "did you have something casual going with Jack too?"

Ashley turned sharply. "Something casual?"

"Dating, sort of dating, friends with non-sexual benefits?"

Ashley raised an eyebrow.

"Light's green."

She accelerated. Popped her gum. "No," she said.

"That's it?"

"No, I didn't?"

Maggie grinned.

"Why, is there a Jackson's Girlfriends Club?"

"Guess it's a small club. Sam and I."

"Really? He was dating you both?"

"Nothing formal or defined, but yeah."

"What a cad."

Maggie shrugged.

"So are you two not enthralled with each other either?"

"We're fine."

Ashley nodded. Maggie said nothing, just smirked. "What?" Ashley finally asked.

"I don't know. I just got the feeling the way he talked about you, that maybe it wasn't all P.I. and cop between you."

"What do you mean how he talked about me? He talked about me to you?"

"No, not really. Just when he mentioned your name. I don't know, I got the feeling he maybe liked you."

"No. Nothing I knew of. And it was just friendly from my side."

"Okay."

Ashley squinted across the SUV at Maggie. She seemed skeptical. Whatever.

"I'm sorry," Maggie said after a minute.

"It's fine."

They drove a little ways.

"So you and Jackson, still 'sort of dating'?"

"Not even that."

Ashley waited, but Maggie said nothing more. That was fine. This wasn't the junior high hallway. And she didn't really care.

The State Police building was connected to the *Procuraduría General de la Republica*—the Attorney General of the Republic. "Do you find the lines between levels of government blurred around here?" Ashley asked as she parked in front of a white iron fence.

"Thank goodness, I thought it was just me."

"Maybe we should have dragged Hillary along."

"We'll manage," Maggie said with a sly grin, and they got out. The clouds had mostly cleared, and the air was warm but pleasant, much clearer than the day before.

It took them a few minutes to find their way once inside, but eventually they were led into the office of a First Sergeant Gallego, a pudgy, clean-shaven man who didn't look much over twenty-one. But he had the stripes to prove his authority. He offered Ashley and Maggie seats and listened as Ashley briefly explained who they were and why they were there—in English, mercifully.

"So you are looking for information about your missing friend, is that it?"

"Yes, and we know the state police spotted his car last night or this morning. We're wondering if there is anything else you can tell us?"

"You are a detective from Los Angeles?" he asked.

"I'm from Redding. She's from Los Angeles."

Sergeant Gallego had studied Ashley's badge briefly already. Now he nodded. "I will give you whatever information we have."

"Thank you."

He smiled, leaned forward, and then held out his hand.

Ashley sighed. "How much?"

"How does one hundred American sound?"

"Like highway robbery."

Gallego shrugged.

"How about we hear the information first?" Maggie said.

The crooked cop curled his fingers inward a few times.

"Or we could pay first," Ashley said, reaching into her pocket. She pulled out three twenty-dollar bills. "That's all I have."

Gallego turned to Maggie.

"I wish Jackson was here right now," she said.

Gallego smiled.

"He'd feed you your sergeant's stripes," she said, digging for forty dollars from her pocket.

"Thank you. Please wait here." He left them in the office and slipped out.

"Any chance he comes back?" Maggie asked.

"Oh, he'll come back. Just might be with a few buddies and handcuffs."

"Good thing we brought a lawyer to Mexico."

Ashley sighed. "Yeah."

*   *   *

11:25 a.m.

HILLARY DREW guard duty. She hung around the pharmacy under the auspices of looking for something until the charade was obvious. Then she browsed T-shirts at the souvenir store next to the tattoo parlor, wincing at the music emanating from within its dark cavern. When she'd fingered just about every knickknack and analyzed every T-shirt slogan in the store, she wandered to the end of the block, purchased an iced lemonade from the cantina, and lingered under an umbrella at an outdoor table.

All the while, she kept her eyes on the door of Room 214 at *El Saguaro*, on Jackson's Granada, on the office and the café. Jackson didn't show. She took a moment to cross the street and wander to the pool, where a woman in a muumuu and two little children were playing in the water. The area was otherwise vacant, and she returned across the street.

Jackson still didn't show.

Sam and Connie were making a figure eight around the block, asking at local shops and bars and hotels, on the off chance Jackson had found a favorite watering hole—or a cute Mexican girl selling trinkets and henna tattoos. It was getting hot and this had long gotten ridiculous.

Hillary's phone rang, and she drew it from her pocket with a sip on her lemon ice. It was Brian. She swiped the screen and lifted the phone to her ear. "Hi, Brian."

"Hey, Babe. Where are you?"

Hillary wasn't wild about the term "Babe," but couldn't seem to dissuade her fiancé from using it. Such was being in love.

"Why do you ask?"

"I stopped by your apartment and you weren't there. And work said you weren't in yesterday."

Hillary sighed. "I'm in Mexico, Brian."

"Mexico? You running away?" He was joking, mostly.

"No. Look, it's complicated, okay? I'm not running away, I'm not in trouble, it has nothing to do with you."

"Okay."

"I'll explain when I get back."

"When are you getting back?"

"I don't know yet. Hopefully tomorrow."

"All right. You're okay?"

"I'm fine, Bri. I'll call you tomorrow night, okay?"

"Okay, Babe. Tomorrow."

She ended the call, sighing at the hurt she heard in his voice. It was bad enough that she was keeping secrets, but to not have told him her plans beforehand was a bad look—not the sort of thing married people did. Worse yet, she wasn't sure why she hadn't told him. So he wouldn't worry? Because she didn't want to admit she was chasing after her first fiancé's troubled brother? Or did it have something to do with Jackson's furtive pleas for her not to marry Brian?

She sighed again. They needed to find Jackson so she could wring his neck, get some straight answers from him, and then forever discard him from her life.

*　　　　*　　　　*

11:47 a.m.

IT TOOK a while, but Gallego returned—sans handcuffs. "I have bad news," he said, sitting down behind his desk again.

"How bad?" Maggie asked.

"Is this your friend?" he asked, spinning a photograph around so they could see it. Ashley exhaled when she looked down at a mugshot, not a headshot from the morgue. It showed Jackson looking glassy-eyed yet intense, dried blood running from a cut above his left eye, another on his lower lip, and general bruising on his face.

"That's him," Maggie breathed.

"He was arrested for public intoxication and getting in a fight with several local men."

"When?" Ashley asked.

"September the twenty-second."

"Four days after he left Tijuana," Maggie said.

"What happened?"

"Well, that is the bad news," Gallego said. "The State Attorney General's office charged him, he was arraigned, and released on twenty thousand peso bail, equal to about one thousand American."

"When's his trial?" Ashley asked, ready to speed-dial Hillary.

"A date has not been set."

"But he was released," Maggie said.

"Yes."

"How serious of a crime is this?" Ashley asked. "I'm surprised this came to the attention of the state police?"

"The fight injured two men quite seriously, and also involved two female tourists from the United States."

Ashley and Maggie exchanged a glance.

"They were not seriously hurt. They appeared to be targets."

"Targets?" Ashley asked. "Targets of whom?"

"According to your friend, of the two men he fought."

"Who were these women?"

"I'm sorry, their names are confidential."

Ashley sighed. "What about the two guys he fought?"

"Local bandits, by the looks of things. They were also released on bail."

"Names?"

Gallego pursed his lips, then held out his hand.

"Forget it," Maggie said. "It's public record."

"True."

"Is that it?" Ashley asked.

"No, that is not it," Gallego said, his lips turning in an evil smile. "Your friend's arrest drew the attention of Judge Benedicto Bautista, a very tough, some say cruel, judge."

"Was he the judge presiding over his arraignment?" Ashley asked.

"Eventually."

"Eventually?" Maggie asked.

"Yes. When he was arrested, your friend had a receipt for a restaurant in his pocket." Gallego slid them another photo, showing the back of a standard restaurant receipt. Three lines of text were scrawled on the back:

Good time – Magdalena Bautista

646-347-4875

"Fumígeno!"

Maggie sat back. "Smoking," she said with an eye roll.

"A rather vulgar American term," Gallego said. "Magdalena Bautista is the daughter of Judge Bautista."

"Oh boy."

"She also has a reputation for being somewhat, um, I believe the term would be 'loose.' She particularly likes American men."

Maggie blinked slowly.

"And Judge Bautista inserted himself in the case when he found out?" Ashley asked.

"Something like that."

"So where do things stand now?"

"Until a date for the trial is set, your friend is a free man."

"Why would Judge Bautista release him for such a low amount?" Maggie asked. "Was he bound by law to do so?"

"One thousand dollars American is not low."

"If he's cruel and was angry it was."

"I suppose. No, he was not obligated, and I am not sure why he did. But he did give your friend a rather stern warning to stay away from Magdalena."

"Can you tell us where we can find her?"

"I cannot give out that information."

"What about the receipt? Can you tell us the restaurant?"

"Of course. *Muy Picante.* It's a small place by the marina. Excellent food."

"Thanks." Ashley turned to Maggie, who was expressionless. "Is there anything else you can tell us?" she asked Gallego.

"I think you have about one hundred dollars' worth."

Ashley forced the words "Thank you" out her lips, and she and Maggie stood and saw themselves out.

"Something not sound right about all this?" Maggie asked.

"Something? Try everything."

"Why would a corrupt judge with a grudge let Jackson out cheaply?"

"I don't know."

"If he gets back across the border, we're not extraditing over beating up some bandits, are we?"

"I don't know."

Maggie sighed.

"Let's go get some lunch."

"Got a place in mind?"

"In fact I do."

Chapter Eleven

12:33 p.m.

THE NEXT TIME Connie came to Mexico, she was packing more comfortable shoes. She had followed Sam for what felt like miles, listening—when she could understand them—to Sam's questions. Nobody had seen Jackson, knew of Jackson, or—in some cases—even had the time to talk to two "*gringos*." She was pretty sure that was the term, although maybe that only applied to men. Or cowboys.

Connie sighed with relief when she and Sam rounded the corner and she saw that garish green cactus on the hideous wall of *El Saguaro*. Who had the bright idea to name a hotel after something pokey and prickly anyhow?

Hillary stood out like the proverbial sore thumb, in her beauty, her height—at six feet, she towered over most of the local women—and her hair. Even with the tourists, she was one of a kind on the streets of Ensenada. She held a mostly empty cup of something cold and refreshing looking, and reported there had been no sign of Jackson.

"We didn't find anything either," Sam said. "Either he's kept a low profile or people can't remember a face."

"Goodness, can you remember all the faces that come through the ER?" Connie asked. "I see hundreds at a day at the DMV, and they all blur."

"Maggie called," Hillary said. "Asked us to meet them at *Muy Picante*."

"Very Spicy," Sam translated.

"Young people and their foods," Connie muttered.

"Did she say if they'd found anything?" Sam asked.

"Said she'd brief us when we got there."

94

"Where is it?"

"On Miramar. A few blocks west."

Hillary led the way, and Connie tried not to grumble about more walking. They crossed the main highway, passing a McDonald's, a Starbucks, and a GNP. At a 7-Eleven, they turned left—west—on a narrow road that looked more like an alley. After the first intersection and a small parking area, they found themselves enclosed by a wall on the left and a row of hole-in-the-wall eating establishments on the right. It initially had a seedy feel, but Connie realized if this was a food truck festival back in L.A., people would stand in line for the food. And they were doing so here too, and at a market beyond the wall on the left. And despite the cramped and crowded conditions, the various establishments looked clean.

Hillary stopped in front of *Muy Picante*, which featured a sign above the entrance with the name and lots of pictures of peppers. There was no door, just two wide openings to a seating area with five or six picnic tables, covered in bright orange tablecloths, each with a variety of sauce bottles and a tube of paper towels in the center. Off to one side was a tiny counter with a menu above it, no doubt in Spanish. Connie was suddenly pining for a cool drink from Starbucks or even McDonald's.

"It's been five minutes," Sam said.

"Probably had trouble parking," Hillary said. Then she nodded. Connie and Sam both turned to see Ashley and Maggie weaving through the crowd. They didn't seem to be bursting with good news.

"You find anything?" Ashley asked.

Sam shook her head. "Nothing."

"And he didn't show up?" Ashley asked.

"No," Hillary said. "What'd you find?"

"Let's eat and talk."

"Here?" Connie asked.

"Good as anywhere," Maggie said.

"I guess."

There weren't many options on the menu at *Muy Picante*, and they ranged on a scale from lava to something called *el aburrido burrito*, which Connie was informed meant the boring burrito—boring as in not spicy at all. They ordered, and took food on throwaway plastic plates with throwaway plastic utensils and those red cups college kids used at drinking parties—or so Connie had heard—to an isolated picnic table.

Hillary had barely sat down before she asked again, "What'd you find?"

Ashley and Maggie took turns explaining how they had bribed Sergeant Gallego for info, and what he had told them about Jackson's second arrest in as many weeks in Mexico.

"So he's at large now?" Connie asked, testing her burrito.

"Something like that," Ashley said. "We should have left a note on his car or something."

"You think he'd return a handwritten note but not a phone call?" Hillary asked.

"If he knew we were down here, yeah."

"Isn't it clear this isn't the same Jackson we all know and love?"

"All?" Maggie asked before taking a bite of her burrito.

Hillary sighed. "Was it his handwriting, on the receipt?"

Maggie swallowed. "Looked like it."

"So what, he comes here to get a couple *flamaente fajitas* and also ask where to pick up a 'smoking hot' local girl?"

"Can you not use the term local girl?" Sam said with a wince.

"If the slinky dress fits . . ."

"She's not a local girl," Ashley said. "Maggie actually Googled her on the drive back."

"She's on Google?" Sam asked as she reached for her cup.

"She has something of a reputation, Ensenada's version of a Kardashian, famous for being famous. Had a failed singing career, a failed relationship with a local surfing sensation, and is now mostly known for hitting up the Ensenada club scene and looking for hot American guys."

"My goodness, what would Jackson want with her?" Connie asked.

"When was all this?" Sam asked.

"Almost a month ago. September 22."

"A Sunday?"

"Yes."

"And nothing since?"

"Right," Maggie said.

"But his car's at the hotel. Is it possible it's been sitting there since then?"

"Possible," Ashley said, reaching for a second taco.

"So where is Jackson?" Connie asked.

"Wait, you said the judge just let him off the hook?" Sam asked.

"Not off the hook," Ashley said, "but certainly didn't throw the book at him."

"Why would he do that?" she asked Hillary.

She dabbed her mouth with a napkin before answering. "He probably wouldn't, not if he's the sort of judge Gallego suggested. Even if he was a straight judge, Jackson is the epitome of a flight risk. It doesn't make sense."

"That's what we thought," Maggie said.

"You think he's done something to him?" Sam asked. "Off the record, to punish him for being interested in his daughter?"

"It's possible," Ashley said.

"But from what we hear of Magdalena Bautista," Maggie said, "he'd have to punish half the guys in Ensenada."

"Well, what do we do?" Connie asked, wiping her hands on her napkin. "Where to now?"

"Here," Ashley said. "We'll ask around, see if anybody remembers giving Jackson Magdalena's name. If so, maybe they can tell us more about his state of mind, if he was really looking for a smoking date or had some other reason for tracking her down."

"The names of the bandits who got in the fight with him are public record, so we could try to find them," Maggie said. "But I don't know that that leads anywhere."

"What about Judge Bautista?" Hillary asked.

"You want to question the judge?" Ashley asked.

"Worth a try. I've been known to twist a few judges' arms over the years," she said with a smirk.

"And we should try to talk to Magdalena too."

"Busy afternoon," Sam said.

Maggie had practically wolfed down her burrito and rice. "Let's get to it then."

"You mind if we swallow first?" Ashley asked.

"You keep eating. I'll ask around."

"See if you can find a bathroom, dear," Connie said as she stood. "This *aburrido burrito* isn't as *aburrido* as they claim."

*   *   *

1:58 p.m.

MAGGIE'S INQUIRIES at *Muy Picante* had turned up nothing. Nobody there recognized Jackson's name or photo, remembered writing down Magdelana's number for him, or even admitted to knowing her other than by reputation. They certainly weren't close enough to her to be giving out her digits to strangers. But, as Hillary had pointed out, he could have easily gotten the name from a fellow patron at the restaurant, or even used the receipt as scratch paper much later in the day.

After eating, the group had walked back to *El Saguaro*. Jackson's car was still there. They had then booked a west-facing room at the Best Western a little down the street but still with a view of his car. It didn't have room for all of them to sleep, unless they doubled in beds and used the floor or armchair, but it gave them a place to get out of the heat of the day, take a load off, and do some research—while keeping an eye on Jackson's car, should he happen to return.

Ashley and Maggie teamed up to dive into the local public records, looking for anything on the arrest that had not been part of Gallego's narrative. Hillary researched Judge Benedicto Bautista—his history as a judge, his rulings, and allegations of misconduct. That left Sam to do a deeper dive on Magdalena Bautista while Connie—and occasionally Ashley—kept a watch out for Jackson.

Magdalena was pretty, but in the photos Sam found, that beauty was obscured by too much makeup and ostentatious outfits that never quite concealed enough of certain places. There wasn't much more to her history than what Maggie had found and disclosed at lunch. Sam's search of her social media profiles didn't get very far, and didn't reveal anything other than more photos like she'd already found and Magdalena's appetite for young men, mostly Caucasian, and alcohol. Tequila shots seemed to be her favorite.

Shortly before two, they gathered to brief each other. There hadn't been much to find on the bandits, a couple of repeat offenders named Alberto Flores and Nick Herrera. They'd been busted for pickpocketing, theft, aggravated assault, and public intoxication previously, and since the incident on the twenty-second, Flores had subsequently been arrested again for theft and was currently in jail. Herrera was at large. The group agreed that even if they found Herrera or managed to talk to Flores, they would be able to tell them little about Jackson's current whereabouts or situation. The names of the two female tourists who had been Flores and Herrera's target weren't available to the public, so by unanimous vote, that was declared a dead end.

Hillary's report on Judge Bautista backed up Gallego's statement that he was a tough, no-nonsense judge known for giving some of the harshest rulings and sentences. She didn't find any other instances of him showing leniency in so much as setting bail, which made his treatment of Jackson that much odder. And while there weren't any official records of Bautista misbehaving, he did have a reputation both for his temper and for stepping over the lines separating the branches of government in the state of Baja California. In short, he was not the guy you wanted overseeing your case if you were in the wrong.

Sam revealed what she'd found about Magdalena Bautista, and then the group voted on what to do next. Magdalena was listed in the phonebook with an address north of town, just off the main highway. Satellite images weren't the highest quality, but from what they could tell, it looked like one of the nicer establishments in Ensenada. Then again, that wasn't saying a ton. Ashley and Sam planned to go try to talk to Magdalena, hoping the combination of Sam's sweetness and Ashley's badge could compel her to give answers.

Hillary, with her legal prowess, was going to try to talk to Judge Bautista. Maggie was going with her, while Connie was going to remain at the Best Western, just in case Jackson happened to return. Shortly before two-thirty, they split up and headed out again. Since the Rogue had been rented in Ashley's name, she and Sam took it while the other two called for a cab.

The drive back north from Ensenada was even more scenic than in the morning. Unfortunately, Sam couldn't enjoy the scenery. She didn't know what to make of what they had learned that afternoon, but she knew it wasn't good.

Magdalena's apartment building stood on the coast side of the highway, on a bluff overlooking the beach. Clean white walls, sharp lines, and plenty of glass lined with bright blue trim—same color as the doors and balcony railings—gave the building a sleek and modern look. Ashley parked in a visitor section of the lot, and she and Sam got out.

"You take the lead," Ashley said.

"What? The lead?"

"My take on Magdalena Bautista is she isn't going to be terribly forthcoming with a couple of white chicks from the States. So I want to save dropping my badge on the table as a last resort."

"Okay. Will your badge do anything down here?"

"We'll see."

"What do I say?"

"Tell her the truth and ask her the questions we've been asking."

"Okay," Sam said with a nod.

The lobby was airy and cool, with a beach theme. Sam and Ashley found a directory and identified Magdalena's room on the top floor.

"Oh crap," Ashley said.

"What?"

"Apartment thirteen."

"So?"

Ashley bit down on her tongue. "I'm sort of . . . not a fan of the number . . ."

"Thirteen?"

"Yeah."

"What do you mean not a fan?"

"I mean I'm terrified of it." She raked her hand through her hair. "I know it's absurd, okay? I have a phobia. Triskaidekaphobia."

"You're serious?"

"Yes," Ashley said, stomping her foot. "I'm not even superstitious. I just . . . I don't know."

Sam nodded, trying to figure out how someone could be afraid of a number. Superstitions, she sort of understood, but fear of the number?

"You may really have to take the lead, say if I break out in a cold sweat or something."

"Has that happened before?"

"Once, on an investigation. Dylan had to interview a witness while I sat in the car."

"Do you need to sit in the car now?"

"I don't know. This is so stupid."

"How do you manage the day between the twelfth and fourteenth of every month? How are you making it through this year?"

"It's fine if I don't have to interact with the number. So I don't make appointments on that day, don't buy items with certain prices, stupid stuff like that. But entering an apartment . . . Sam, this is so embarrassing."

"What do you want to do?"

Ashley took a deep breath. "Go talk to her."

"Me?"

"No, us. It's just an apartment. It isn't going to hurt me. Let's do this."

"Okay."

"Just be ready to catch me if faint."

Chapter Twelve

2:43 p.m.

SAM AND ASHLEY took the elevator, and Sam led the way to Apartment 13. She rang the bell and looked at Ashley, who appeared as if she was going to be sick.

The door swung halfway open, and a young Latina woman poked her head around it. It was not Magdalena, although she bore a resemblance to her. Same flawless caramel skin and same luxurious dark hair. Less the excessive makeup. She wore a flared-sleeve blouse and designer jeans, no shoes. Gold bangles on her wrist matched a necklace and small hoop earrings. She was nicely dressed, but not showy.

"Yes? Can I help you?" she asked in Spanish.

Sam replied accordingly. "We're looking for Magdalena. Is she here?"

"No, she is in Cabo San Lucas for the weekend. Are you friends of hers?"

"Friends of a friend, we think," Sam said. She introduced herself and Ashley, who managed a feeble wave. "We were hoping to ask her about a man named Jackson Douglas, who we think she may have known."

"Jackson Douglas?" the woman asked, her almond brown eyes widening.

"Do you know him?"

"I do. Would you like to come in?"

"Thank you," Sam said.

The woman swung the door all the way open and Sam followed her. So did Ashley, albeit as if half paralyzed. The apartment was spacious and airy, with one entire wall made of glass and looking out over a balcony at the Pacific. The woman offered Sam and Ashley seats on a white loveseat facing a glass coffee table in a living room a step down from the entry, the kitchen, and a hallway leading presumably to bedrooms.

"Would you prefer to speak English?" the woman asked, still in Spanish.

"Please," Sam said, in English.

The woman sat down in a chair adjacent to the couch. "I'm Mariana Bautista," she said. "Magdalena is my older sister. We share the apartment."

"And you know Jackson Douglas?"

"I do."

"This Jackson Douglas?" Ashley asked. She sat tentatively on the edge of the loveseat, but had rallied enough to retrieve her phone and show Mariana a photo.

"Yes, that's him."

"How do you know him?" Sam asked.

"I am—or should say, was—his tutor."

"His tutor?"

"I was teaching him to speak Spanish. He is taking classes at *Universidad Xochicalco*, but his Spanish is not very good."

"Classes? What kind of classes?"

"He seemed to be studying our history, our culture, the language and customs of Mexico."

Sam looked to Ashley. The same courses a person might take if they were planning to relocate somewhere.

"When did you first meet him?" Sam asked.

"About a month ago? I do not remember the exact date. He called me on a Thursday afternoon, and we met the following Saturday for a first 'session.'"

"How many times did you meet?"

"Just twice. That Saturday and then the following Friday evening. I was disappointed he did not contact me again," she said with a shrug. "I liked working with him. I kind of liked him." Her smile vanished. "One of you is not his girlfriend, are you?"

"No," Ashley said. Sam shook her head.

Mariana leaned on the arm of the chair, running her hand through her hair. "Jackson was sweet and funny, and his Spanish was so bad," she said with a laugh. "We flirted a little, and I thought maybe, one day, we would go beyond tutor and student." She shrugged. "So when I didn't hear anything more from him, I was disappointed, like I said."

"Did you try calling him?" Sam asked.

Mariana shook her head.

"Did he say anything about where he might be going or doing next?"

"No. He seemed interested in learning Spanish and . . . having fun doing it."

"Did he say why he was in Mexico, why he was taking classes?"

"Not really," Mariana said after a moment's thought. "He said he had relocated from Los Angeles, that he wanted a change."

"He said the word 'relocated'?" Sam asked.

"Yes, I think that was the word."

"Can you remember the dates you met with him?" Ashley asked.

"Let me think. It was the last Friday in September, so then the Saturday before that."

"Twenty-seventh and twenty-first," Ashley said after consulting her phone.

"That sounds right."

"Did he say anything to you about being arrested?"

"Arrested?"

"Sunday the twenty-second, he got into a fight stopping some bandits from robbing a couple tourists."

"No, he didn't say anything. I can't believe it. Stopping bandits?"

Ashley nodded.

"So he's a hero?"

"Back home too."

"Mariana," Sam said, "the police said your father was the judge who set Jackson's bail."

"My father?"

"Apparently he was called in because Jackson had your sister's name on a slip of paper in his pocket."

"My sister. She didn't say anything about knowing him."

"Did you mention him to her?" Ashley asked.

"No. My sister's social life puts mine to shame. She dates more guys in a week than I do in a year. And I tutor quite a lot of people—it's a side job for me while I go to school—so Jackson did not stand out in that regard."

"Do you attend . . . where was it?" Sam asked.

"*Universidad Xochicalco.* No, I go to UABC, just up the road. But I advertise at *Xochicalco.* It's how Jackson found me."

"That makes sense," Sam said. At least as much sense as anything was making.

"You said he had Maggie's number?" Mariana asked.

"Maggie?"

"My sister."

"Right, sorry. Yes, on the back of a receipt from a little place on Miramar called *Muy Picante.*"

"I think I've heard of it. Look, like I said, my sister gets around. Almost anyone could have given him her number. And for all I know, she might have dated him and just not told me." She sighed. "Maybe that's why he stopped contacting me, because he was seeing her."

Sam wanted to comfort Mariana by telling her that probably wasn't the case, but the alternative wasn't much more heartening. So she turned to Ashley to see if she had any more questions for her.

"Mariana," she said, "we're trying to track down Jackson. He was staying at a hotel on *Avenue Adolfo López Mateos* but missed his checkout this morning, left his car in the lot, and we have no idea where he is. Your tutoring date with him on the twenty-seventh is the most recent we've heard of him. Is there anything else you can think of that might give us a clue?"

Mariana thought for close to thirty seconds. "I don't think so, I'm sorry. We kept our conversation pretty light."

Ashley nodded.

"You said he was staying on *Avenue Adolfo López Mateos?*"

"For a month."

"We met there."

"You met there?"

"Well, not at the hotel. But at a little café he said he'd discovered. The Cactus."

Ashley nodded again. "That's the hotel he was staying at."

"Really? He never said that."

Ashley retrieved a business card from her pocket. "If you think of anything else, no matter how insignificant, will you call me?"

"Of course," Mariana said. "I'm sorry I cannot be of more help. And I hope he's all right."

They thanked her and exited the apartment and turned for the elevator.

"You did good," Ashley said.

"So did you. In apartment thir—"

"Don't say it, but thanks."

"Unfortunately, we didn't learn much."

"We need to touch base with *Universidad Xochicalco*, see if Jackson was really taking classes there. I can't believe he was, unless their semester starts really late. Even so, I can't believe it."

"Why would he put up a front to Mariana?"

"Really? To get a pretty girl."

"But why Mariana?" Sam asked as they stepped into the elevator. "To get close to Magdalena? Or was it the other way around?"

"I don't know. But this just gets weirder and weirder."

"It's almost like he's living two lives. Drunk, brawling, going to bullfights, and the sweet, funny student trying to assimilate to Mexico."

"I was thinking the same thing."

The elevator dinged and the doors opened.

Sam sighed. "And we still have no clue where he is."

*   *   *

2:50 p.m.

MAGGIE COULDN'T help notice the Pemex sign next to the blocky green and white building where the cab dropped them off. Her last trip to Mexico had been to expose a man named Leonardo Vasquez, who had discovered tons of crude oil and used all manner of corruption in an effort to privatize the oil business (away from Pemex, the Mexican government-owned petroleum company) and make millions. Back then, she had still been making her bones with the *Los Angeles Times*, and Jackson had come to her rescue. Now, she realized as she and Hillary got out of the cab, the roles were reversed.

White lettering on the side of the building read *Poder Judicial Del Estado Juzgados Civiles*, which roughly translated to the civil court for the state. Fenced in, like everything in Mexico, the building was new and modern, with lots of glass and fronted by palm trees in a rock garden. Maggie had already told Hillary she was following her lead, and now did so literally. The inside of the building was cool and professional, and Maggie wondered how much of that was to give an appearance of legitimacy and how much of it had been purchased by corruption. Her minimal experience had confirmed what she'd always heard—the Mexican criminal system was as crooked as the Rio Grande.

Hillary had done some brief research, and had informed Maggie on the ride over that Mexico's thirty-one states each had a three-part system of government with an executive, legislative, and judicial branch. The judicial branch, much like in the U.S., had a supreme court, appellate courts, and the court of first instance that heard civil, criminal, and commercial cases. Contrary to U.S. trials by jury, criminal cases in Mexico were decided by a judge. Precedent—or case law—was not valued to the extent it was in America, but rather, in Mexico, judges referred back to long-observed codes and customs. And in Mexico, the accused was considered guilty until proven innocent. From Maggie's point of view, the system basically begged judges to be corrupt, and they readily obliged.

A young secretary dressed like a call girl manned a front desk. She spoke enough English for Hillary to converse in her native tongue and ask if they could speak with Judge Bautista. The secretary took their names and asked them to have a seat. The open lobby was a hub of hallways and offices, with several seating areas arranged in the rare places where there was enough wall to do so. Short of plush, the chairs and end tables were at least comfortable and not in a state of disrepair. The plants were real.

The music was soft, Spanish-tinged classical. There were worse places to wait.

Hillary sighed as she flipped through a Spanish magazine, then cast it aside.

"Ask you something?" Maggie said.

"Sure."

"What is it that you hate so much about Jackson?"

"I don't hate Jackson."

"You hide it well."

Hillary sighed again. She crossed her legs and looked at Maggie. "Jackson and I are two different personalities, have two different viewpoints on almost everything, two different ways of going about things. We're the epitome of oil and water. But for all of that, I think we could get along if he wasn't such a waste."

"A waste?"

"Yes. He's smart, funny—if you go for that smart-aleck sort of thing—more clever than I cared to admit, he's relentless when he wants to be. He has the potential to accomplish so much, but all he can think about is soaking up the ocean's ambiance, chilling or 'kickin' it,' hanging out. He responds to everything with a wisecrack, with a nonchalance born of arrogant indifference."

"Wow, tell me how you really feel."

"You asked."

"I did."

Hillary sighed yet again. "And the worst part is, despite all our differences and all the times we've butted heads over the years, we were going to be family. And I did, somewhere deep inside, care for him. So to see him throw his life away makes it that much worse."

"You mean by what we've seen here?"

"I mean as long as I've known him."

"You think he's thrown his life away?"

"He's a private investigator, Maggie."

"So? That's not a legit occupation?"

"Maybe, but not when you pursue it as a tribute to Tom Selleck and James Garner. It's like his entire life is a way to live out his favorite TV shows."

"What about all the good he's done? Saving you, saving me. Protecting Wilbur."

"Who?"

"The World War II vet from his last case."

"I don't know about that one, but in your case, my case, Ashley's case, he came to the rescue of people who got themselves in trouble. I won't deny he acted heroically, but he's always reacting, fixing problems. He never accomplishes anything."

"What should he accomplish?"

"With all his God-given talents, something."

"Maybe he has."

A small, thin man in a rumpled shirt and loose tie approached them. "Miss McKenzie?"

"Yes," Hillary said, standing. Maggie did as well, convinced the man in front of them was not Judge Bautista. "My name is Yuniel Ybarra. I understand you wish to speak to Judge Bautista."

"Yes," Hillary said again.

"Please, come with me."

They followed him down a hallway and to a large office space cordoned off into several cubicles. Ybarra showed them to a desk in the far corner. It featured a modern desktop computer and monitor, photos of Ybarra with a woman and several children, and a shelf full of law reference books. There was also a nameplate identifying Ybarra as a *pasante* or clerk.

After they had all sat down, Ybarra explained, "Judge Bautista is very busy, so it is important that we screen his appointments, especially those who walk in. So please, can you tell me why you'd like to speak to him?"

Hillary recapped the basics for Ybarra, and Maggie was content to let her do so. She spoke eloquently, almost condescendingly. Maggie surmised that Hillary had the ability to insult without offending. Ybarra was not offended, judging by his facial expressions, and he listened attentively. When Hillary was finished, he asked a few questions, then sat back with his hands on the desk.

"So what precisely do you wish to ask His Honor?"

"To be clear," Hillary said, "we're not in any way impugning Judge Bautista or questioning his judgment, but we're hoping he can give us any details about Jackson's alleged crimes, the charges against him, where the legal process stands, and where he may be at present."

Ybarra nodded, as if this all was fair. He then asked them to wait, stood, and disappeared.

"Ask you one more thing?" Maggie said.

"Sure."

"Have you ever lost a case?"

Hillary turned her way. "Why do you ask?"

"Because I would imagine you could persuade just about anybody to do just about anything."

Hillary looked at her.

"I mean that in a good way."

She nodded. "Twice. One was not my fault."

Maggie nodded in return. Then they waited quietly. Somewhere in the large office area, in another cubicle, two people were talking in *muy rapido* Spanish. Maggie probably could have kept up if she'd wanted to, legalese aside, but she had no interest. Elsewhere, someone was typing a mile a minute on a keyboard. There was the hum of an air conditioner, all typical office ambient noise. There was not a ticking clock, which would have been appropriate, given how long Maggie and Hillary waited for Ybarra.

When he returned, his lips were pursed. "I am very sorry, ladies, but Judge Bautista is unavailable today."

"What does unavailable mean?" Hillary asked.

"He is a very busy man, I am afraid. And he has personally told me he knows nothing about your case which he is permitted to reveal to you. I am sorry."

Hillary's experience in the courtroom—or with bureaucracy—must have told her there was no point in pursuing things further, so she didn't protest. Instead, she thanked Ybarra, and she and Maggie headed for the exit. At the curb, where they hoped to hail a taxi, they sidestepped a man in an old sport coat and wrinkled slacks who was smoking a cigarette.

"Now what?" Maggie asked.

"Ask the detective," Hillary said.

"You giving up?"

"I hate losing, but I also know when to cut bait."

"And this is that time?"

"Wouldn't you say?"

Maggie shrugged.

"*Perdóneme,*" the man with the cigarette said, inching toward them, "*¿tienes fuego?*"

"*No. Lo siento.*"

"*Gracias,*" he said, extending a slip of paper to Maggie. She took it reflexively, and he shuffled away. She unfolded it and tipped it to Hillary. Her eyes went from the note to the man, who had wandered a dozen paces away. He casually turned back their way and gave an ever so slight shake of the head when Hillary made as if to speak to him.

Maggie looked back at the note before stuffing it into her pocket. Written in Spanish, it said only *banderas monumentales* and a time, 6:00. Maggie looked at Hillary, who shrugged, then used her phone to call for a cab. It arrived in five minutes, by which time the mysterious man had flicked his unlit cigarette into the street and returned inside the courthouse.

Chapter Thirteen

3:47 p.m.

"MY TURN TO ask you something," Hillary said as they rode in the back of a cab back toward the Best Western.

Maggie turned from looking absentmindedly out the window, wondering about the cloak-and-dagger note passage outside the courthouse. "What's that?"

"Why aren't you and Jackson a couple?"

"Why?" Maggie asked.

"You seem like a match."

Maggie raised an eyebrow. "I think I'm insulted, given your take on Jack earlier."

"I didn't mean like that," Hillary said. "But you're both casual, carefree, witty, don't care what people think if you believe something to be true. You seem like the kind of person who'd like to hang out at the beach, spend the night in an arcade or watching *24* reruns. You're not a high-maintenance girly girl who would drive him nuts."

"What, have you been playing matchmaker for him or something? You seem to have his romantic interests pegged."

"Are you dodging the question?"

"Are you?"

Hillary's eyes flashed for a moment. "Forget I asked," she said, turning away.

Maggie sighed. "Jack and I weren't interested in anything serious, in a match."

"Weren't?"

"I started dating someone else."

"So he wasn't the one not ready?"

"Initially," Maggie said. "But I realized I wasn't either."

"So you're not dating anymore?"

"No."

"And still not interested in Jackson?"

"Why do you want to know?"

Hillary shrugged. "Curiosity."

Maggie wasn't sure she bought that, but went along with it. "I'm not interested in being a girlfriend or a fiancée or anything. And last I talked to Jack, he didn't seem much interested in anything either."

Hillary didn't push the conversation any further, and Maggie turned her head back out the window. She and Russell had dated for a couple of months before she'd realized she wasn't ready for a relationship that went beyond being friends. With him or anybody. Yet she couldn't deny there seemed to be *something* more when she thought about Jackson. She believed that was just past history, his impact on leading her to faith in Christ, his saving her life multiple times. But maybe it was more than that—maybe there was something romantic there. Or should be.

Hillary said something to the driver in Spanish, snapping Maggie's head toward her.

"*Sí, señora.*"

"What did you tell him?" Maggie asked, having not been paying attention.

"I told him to drop us at the movie theater."

"You take a sudden interest in foreign films?"

"We're being followed."

"What?"

"Same black sedan has been on our tail since we left the courthouse."

"You were watching?"

"I happened to see someone get into it while we were waiting for a cab, but it never left the parking lot. Then it pulled out behind us. Still there."

Maggie turned her head halfway to see. Sure enough, a black sedan with no front plate was following them.

"So what, we pull a pizza parlor trick?"

"Something like that. Call Ashley, see if she can arrange to pick us up on the street west of the highway."

Maggie did, and Ashley said she'd leave the hotel immediately.

"Tell her to sit with the doors unlocked, and if we see a tail, we'll keep walking and get back to her."

Maggie related that to Ashley as well, then ended the call. "You think it's someone from the courthouse?"

"Considering the clandestine drop on the sidewalk, yes."

"But why?"

"Because there's more to this story than we thought."

The driver dropped them across the street from the *Cinépolis*, and Maggie and Hillary dodged multiple lanes of traffic to enter a modern, mission-style building identified as *Plaza Marina*, a shopping center that included a theater. Maggie glanced to their left once to see the sedan had pulled over several cars behind the cab. One man got out of the passenger seat. He wore a cheap suit, similar to Ybarra's and the mystery man's.

Maggie followed Hillary, who seemed far more adept at this sort of thing than a high-class defense attorney should be. They hurried through the main hall of the mall and out onto a narrow street on the back side. Ashley's Rogue was parked a few slots down the road, and they were in the backseat in seconds.

"Pull away casually," Hillary said, and Ashley accelerated away from the curb smoothly.

Maggie looked back through tinted windows and didn't see the man in the cheap suit exit the mall until they were most of the way down the block and several other cars had pulled in behind them. Still, Ashley took a roundabout way back to the Best Western, but none of the three women spotted a tail.

Once safely in their room, they related the mini adventure to Sam and Connie, who asked the same questions Maggie and Hillary had been pondering. No one had any answers.

They settled down with cool drinks to report out. Jackson's Granada sat unmoved in the *El Saguaro* lot, and Connie had not seen him, and hadn't moved from her perch except once to use the restroom.

Hillary relayed what they'd learned—or not learned—at the courthouse, along with the secretive note passed to them. She had checked while in the cab, and *banderas monumentales*—or monumental flags—referred to a giant flagpole and Mexican flag by the harbor, one of many throughout Mexico that came about through a presidential program in 1999. It was a public place, before dark, and thus should be fairly safe. But after being tailed from the justice building, they weren't taking anything lightly.

Ashley and Sam then explained their attempt to talk to Magdalena Bautista, their conversation instead with Mariana, and their subsequent calls to *Universidad Xochicalco*, which had no record of anyone named Jackson Douglas ever attending or taking classes.

"Why would he fake that?" Connie asked.

"To get a pretty girl," Hillary said. "Was Mariana pretty?"

"Very," Ashley said.

"So, what," Maggie said, "he's looking for hot Mexican women, gets the name Magdalena from somebody, and strikes out with her so comes up with a ruse to get her sister? And then, after two 'dates,' he cuts and runs?"

"Maybe he got in trouble with the law again," Connie said.

"Or Judge Bautista," Sam said.

"And that's the other thing, these girls just happen to be the daughters of a state judge who has the power to have Jackson . . . what, done away with?"

"That's just it," Ashley said. "We don't know what he's done with him. Or anything."

"Too much coincidence," Maggie said. "Jack hated coincidence."

"What's the alternative, he orchestrated all this?" Hillary asked.

Maggie shrugged.

"To what end?"

She shrugged again.

"We need to talk to your cigarette smoking mystery man," Ashley said. "I'll go with you at six."

"He sees someone other than us, he might spook," Hillary said.

"Then I'll shoot him in the butt."

"You didn't bring a gun, dear," Connie said.

"Dang."

"And if you're followed again?" Sam asked.

"Or he is?" Maggie added.

"We lost a tail once," Hillary said matter-of-factly. "We'll do it again."

"What time is this meeting?" Connie asked.

"Six," Hillary answered.

"Then we have time to eat beforehand. Because that spicy little place in the alley didn't fill me up."

"Probably a good idea," Ashley said. "I have a feeling that if this guy can tell us anything, we may not feel like eating after we hear it."

*   *   *

5:55 p.m.

ASHLEY LOOKED up at a twenty-five-meter by fourteen-meter red, white, and green flag floating languidly in the evening breeze from atop a fifty-meter-tall flagpole. Contrary to the night before, the sky behind the flag was bright and clear, free of haze. Beyond the pole, which sat in a paved circle by the harbor, was the open water and the port, currently housing a Carnival cruise ship, with its distinctive red and blue whale tailfin, and a container ship being loaded by giant cranes.

Ashley stood between Hillary and Maggie, the sounds and smells of sidewalk vendors all around them. This was the main tourist section of Ensenada, and this was prime tourist time—just before sunset. After two full days in Mexico, Ashley was tired of it all—tourist or not—and ready to go home. But first, they had a job to finish.

They'd eaten takeout from McDonald's, tired of cheap Mexican food and not in the mood to savor some of the finer cuisine the city may have had to offer. While Connie and Sam remained in the hotel room to keep a vigil on *El Saguaro's* parking lot and to avoid overwhelming the potential informant, Ashley, Hillary, and Maggie had walked the several blocks to the *banderas monumentales*. They had not observed any signs of being tailed or watched.

A cab pulled to the curb and a man in dark pants and an untucked short-sleeve dress shirt got out. He had somewhat wavy black hair, and looked furtively around as he exited. So did Ashley, but she didn't spot any signs that the cab had been pursued. The guy paid the driver and walked toward them. Already, Ashley could tell by Hillary and Maggie's change in posture that this was the guy who had passed Maggie the note earlier.

"Thank you for meeting me," he said when he reached them. Although he did not seem in the least put off by Ashley's presence, Hillary introduced them all by first name.

"My name is Mauricio Chávez," he said with a thick accent, but in solid English. "I am a clerk in Judge Bautista's office."

"Why did you want to meet with us?" Hillary asked.

"I overheard you speaking with *Señor* Ybarra. You have questions about a friend of yours, *Señor* Douglas?"

"We do," Hillary said.

"Let us walk and talk," he said. They proceeded toward the flagpole, toward the water's edge. "I slipped you the paper because I should not be talking with you. If Judge Bautista were to find out, I would lose my job— or worse."

"Then why are you talking with us?" Maggie asked.

"Because you should know the truth, for your own good."

"What's the truth?" Ashley asked.

"I am afraid, not good. *Señor* Douglas is gone."

"Gone?" Maggie asked.

"Let me explain." They turned past a clamshell-shaped amphitheater and ventured north on a sidewalk beside the marina. "When *Señor* Douglas was arrested last month, and Magdalena Bautista's name was found in his possession, the state police contacted Judge Bautista. It is no trouble in our legal system for someone like Judge Bautista to assert his influence and become the presiding judge in a case. The judge had a meeting with *Señor* Douglas and warned him to have no contact with Magdalena whatsoever."

"That's it?" Hillary asked.

"It was a very serious threat. He backed it up by having Jackson 'roughed up' by some members of the police."

"How does something like that fly?" Maggie asked.

"Fly?"

"How is it allowed?" Hillary asked.

"This is Mexico."

"Then what?" Ashley asked.

"Less than a week later, *Señor* Douglas was arrested again, this time by the Federal Police."

"He was arrested again?"

"Yes."

"For what?" Hillary asked.

"He started a fight at a local bar. Nearly killed two men."

"A fight over what?" Maggie asked after several paces. She was the first of the three women to find words.

"From what I hear, these men were human traffickers. Whether *Señor* Douglas knew this or not, I do not know. Given the nature of the crime, the federal police were contacted. One of the men *Señor* Douglas beat up is still in the hospital, in a coma."

"Why would he do that?" Ashley asked.

"I do not know," Chávez answered. "These were very bad men, but I do not know what provoked your friend.

"What happened to him?" Hillary asked.

"He appeared before Judge Bautista again. The judge was irate. You have to understand, he is a very corrupt man, and was likely receiving kickbacks from the traffickers."

"Seriously?" Maggie asked.

"I do not know of a paper trail to prove this, but yes, I believe it to be true. Judge Bautista has his hands in every pot. He also had been informed that *Señor* Douglas had been seeing his other daughter, Mariana. Someone had sent him photographs of the two of them together. In one, *Señor* Douglas gave her some money. In another, they were walking toward a hotel. It looked very bad."

"Which hotel?" Ashley asked.

"I do not recall."

"We talked to Mariana," Maggie said. "She told us she had been tutoring Jackson."

"Judge Bautista asked *Señor* Douglas about these photos. He only smirked."

"You were there?"

Chávez nodded.

"So what happened?" Ashley asked.

"Judge Bautista was livid. Magdalena Bautista is known to be a flirt. But Mariana is sweet and innocent. And these photographs seemed to be showing *Señor* Douglas, uh, excuse me, paying for her services."

"She was tutoring him," Maggie repeated.

Chávez shrugged. "*Señor* Douglas said nothing about this. He only smirked again and told Judge Bautista that he had been warned away from Magdalena, not Mariana."

Ashley exhaled.

"Judge Bautista was very red. He approached *Señor* Douglas within inches of his face and said he had broken the law several times within a short span, with escalating violence. Furthermore, he had been warned to leave Mexico and warned to leave Judge Bautista's daughter alone. He threatened to have him thrown into prison for the rest of his life, that the charges merited it. *Señor* Douglas said he would not dare, that he was an American citizen and that Judge Bautista was a fat, old thug who couldn't even keep his young daughter from dating an American criminal. At this, Judge Bautista lost it. He ordered *Señor* Douglas beaten. Then, he gave him one more chance, asking if he had anything to say for himself."

"What did he say?" Maggie asked in dread.

"'*El corazón quiere lo que el corazón quiere.*' The heart wants what the heart wants."

"My goodness," Hillary said.

"I thought Judge Bautista would strangle *Señor* Douglas himself. Instead, he ordered him sent to *Cinco Picos.*"

"Five Peaks?"

"Yes. It is a privately run prison in the state of Sonora, north of Hermosillo. The mountains beyond it have five, distinct peaks. The prison is also shaped like a star, with five points."

"So Jackson's there?" Ashley asked.

"Yes. But I must warn you, *Cinco Picos Prisión* is a very bad place. Those there are known as *los olvidados*—the forgotten. Men who are sent there are as if they are erased from society."

"He can't be erased or forgotten," Ashley said. "He hasn't had a trial."

"This is Mexico," Chávez said again. "Our criminal system is way behind, and that is in instances where we legitimately seek justice. Judge Bautista is not interested in justice, not in this case. He could have the trial delayed or completely forgotten about. He could have *Señor* Douglas deleted from all public records, and he will spend the rest of his life in *Cinco Picos*. He would not be the first person to be forgotten."

"We're not going to let that happen," Ashley said.

"I am sorry, but I do not know if you can stop it. Judge Bautista has already had *Señor* Douglas transferred, and per the law, he is now the property of the prison until such time as a higher court rules otherwise."

"She's a lawyer," Ashley said. "She'll make it happen."

"It will not be easy. Again, this is Mexico."

"You know the truth," Maggie said. "You can help us."

"I am sorry, but I should not have told you what I did. And in fact, Chávez is not my real name. If Judge Bautista knew I had spoken with you, if he knew what I told you, he would kill me and my family."

"We won't tell anyone how we know what we know," Ashley said, "but you have to help us bring the truth to light."

"I am sorry, but I have done all I can. You know all I know. I must go now."

They pleaded with him to reconsider, but he begged off and backed away into the people milling at various shops that lined the walkway. In a minute, he had disappeared, leaving the three women standing alone in the falling gloom.

Chapter Fourteen

Sunday, October 20
12:17 a.m.

SAM WAS IN shellshock. She didn't know what to think, what to believe. Nor could she seem to fit all the pieces together to form a whole—to explain what had happened and why.

She wasn't alone.

Ashley, Hillary, and Maggie had returned from their meeting with "Chávez" and reported what he had told them about Jackson—his third arrest, his smart-aleck replies to Judge Bautista, and his "sentencing" to *Cinco Picos Prisión*. It hadn't seemed possible, even given Jackson's alleged crimes and the man called Chávez's repeated reminder that "this is Mexico," that a man who hadn't been convicted—hadn't even been tried—could be banished to a privately run prison, or that his banishment could be all but permanent. Nor did it seem possible that Jackson could, in the face of that fate, have behaved and responded the way he had.

Unless he had really gone to Mexico "to die," as had originally been suggested.

"Why would he be doing good then?" Maggie had asked.

"Good?" Hillary asked.

"He stopped bandits. He beat up traffickers."

"Sounds to me he was looking for lowlife's to use as a punching bag. He wasn't doing good."

"I think he was crying for help," Connie said. "For someone to notice. First a small crime, then a bigger one, then a bigger one."

"Crying for help," Hillary said, "or punishing himself?"

"Punishing himself?" Sam said.

"Maybe he wanted to get arrested, wanted to get thrown in prison."

"Why would he want that?" Maggie asked.

"Look at all he had to go through to save you twice. Killing people, blowing things up. To save you," she said, nodding at Ashley, "he killed five gangsters. To save me, he killed twenty people. On top of what happened to his family—which he blamed himself for on some level—maybe it was all too much."

"We don't have enough answers still," Ashley said. "And we're not going to get answers until we talk to Jackson."

"Is that possible?" Sam asked.

"There have to be laws," Connie said.

"'This is Mexico,'" Maggie said, mimicking Chávez's accent.

"Main question," Ashley said, "are we done in Ensenada? Do we want to chase down leads here or go to *Cinco Picos*? Or go home?"

"What leads here?" Connie asked.

"Find out more about the bar where he fought the traffickers, get more details about how it started, who these guys were, what else Jackson had been doing. Talk to Mariana again, try to get ahold of Magdalena."

"I say we go to the prison," Maggie said. She nodded at Hillary. "They have to let him see his lawyer."

"But not five lawyers," Hillary said.

"So one. Or one and a paralegal. At least talk to him, get some answers, get his side of the story."

"It's worth a try," Sam said.

"I agree," Connie said.

"Me too," Ashley said, and all four turned to Hillary.

"Let me do some research first. I'm not familiar with Mexican law. We should also research the prison, the roads to get there."

"The roads?" Sam asked.

"Bandits," Maggie said. "Cartels."

"Let's do research," Hillary said. "Then we'll make plans."

So they had done research. Ashley and Hillary had scoured the internet, made phone calls, and called in favors to get more information about *Cinco Picos Prisión* and the legal system in Mexico. They also investigated the seriousness of the charges against Jackson. Meanwhile,

Maggie had called her old source in Mexico City, Anapaula, to see if she or anyone she knew could dig up any more facts about Jackson's arrests, Judge Bautista, or previous people sentenced to *Cinco Picos*. She had also done some of that research herself. Connie had verified the route to the prison, surrounding towns, and safety of travel. And Sam had "floated," helping any of them she could or covering when they adjusted work schedules, notified bosses or friends or loved ones that they might be gone an additional day, or mollified fiancés.

By ten o'clock, they had made the decision to stay the night in Ensenada. Connie had still been researching the specifics of travel warnings issued by the U.S. Department of State along or near the route to the prison. And Hillary had been knee deep in research, e-mailing, texting, and making calls almost simultaneously. The last of Connie's muffins and cookies had been consumed, and Sam was one of several to utilize the beds for a nap—at least until the group had settled on a plan or at least a wake-up hour and time of departure.

Sam slept longer than she intended, and woke up groggily to see that it was quarter after midnight, thus Sunday morning. She took a moment to shake off the cobwebs and remember where she was and what was going on. It made her wish for the cobwebs.

Ashley and Connie were also napping, slouched against the wall and on the other bed, respectively. Hillary stood by the window, a phone to her ear, listening. The door to the balcony was open, and Sam stepped out onto it for some fresh air. Maggie was already there, leaning on the railing, looking over the street. Half the lights and signs of the surrounding stores and restaurants were off. Half were still going—mostly on the bars. Same for the people. The air was still warm, but pleasant.

"Sleep any?" Maggie asked.

"A little."

"Feel better?"

"No."

She nodded.

"What do we know?" Sam asked.

"I don't know what Hillary's found, but I crapped out. My source Anapaula had heard rumors about a 'rogue judge' in Baja California, but no details or confirmation. Nobody else I or she called turned up anything more on Jack. Connie says its fifty-fifty we get hijacked if we try driving to the prison, although I think she was exaggerating."

"Which fifty?" Sam asked.

"Right? Ashley's influence as a detective in northern California apparently doesn't have the pull one would hope down here in Crapico." She paused as Sam winced. "Sorry. Jack's rubbing off on me."

"So we have nothing?"

"Unless Hillary does."

They stayed out a few minutes longer, and when they went in, both Ashley and Connie were stirring. Hillary was at her computer, and said she'd be just a minute. When she was done, and everyone had perked up to some extent, they had another powwow.

Maggie was right, it was not good. In addition to her and Ashley's failures, and Connie's slightly less pessimistic but still cautionary report on travel conditions through the Sonoran Desert, Hillary gave an overview of *Cinco Picos Prisión*. Originally built around the turn of the century, its purpose had been to provide a secure facility to lock up Mexico's worst criminals—cartel members, human traffickers, murderers, rapists. It was run privately in the hopes of keeping governmental corruption out of the process, making it less likely that a poorly paid guard would accept a bribe and look the other way or a corrupt warden would bow to pressure from cartel kingpins. The prison was a fortress and it was guarded by a well-paid private army. Since 2002 when it opened, no one had escaped *Cinco Picos*. Seven men had tried and been shot, and one attempt had been made by a cartel to break out its kingpin. They had all died in the effort without so much as breaching the outer wall.

Since the early 2000s, Mexico's government had made a slight shift in policy regarding the prison. Given its incredibly secure nature, desolate location, and impressive track record at avoiding succumbing to the rampant corruption that plagued every facet of the Mexican government, it became a haven for anyone the government wanted to make disappear. That continued to include cartel members, murderers, and other heinous criminals—the ones Mexico's constitution forbade from being executed.

Sending them to *Cinco Picos* was effectively a death sentence. It was also a place to send criminals the laws of Mexico couldn't properly punish, for one reason or another. They were sent to the desert to be "held" for a time, but that time was indeterminate, and while the prison itself wasn't corrupt, it didn't ask questions about the prisoners it received, and there still existed plenty of corruption in determining which prisoners were sent there. That included political dissidents, despite the aboveboard democratic front presented to the rest of the world, or anyone the government wanted to get rid of but didn't have legal means to do so and for whom there wasn't someone to mount a strong defense.

And, Hillary noted somberly, it sometimes included criminals whom a particular judge disliked, for whatever reason, and wanted to punish. Since criminals in Mexico were considered guilty until proven innocent, and since the legal system was overstressed and overworked and public defenders were even more underpaid than those in the States, it was not uncommon nor all that hard to "lose" someone in the shuffle or sweep him under the rug. And there was no bigger rug in Mexico than *Cinco Picos*.

The bad news didn't stop there. According to Mexican Law, Hillary could no more practice as an attorney in Mexico than any of the other women could. Eventually, with enough research and study, she could learn the nuances of Mexican law and attempt to get licensed in Mexico and thus represent someone in a Mexican court of law. In theory, they could hire a Mexican lawyer, with whom Hillary could work, but only in an unofficial advisory capacity. And from her research, any legitimate Mexican attorney who could be trusted would be a rare find and an expensive hire.

The bottom line was, if Judge Bautista wanted Jackson to be forgotten, he had largely unchecked power and ability to do so, and all indications were he'd done exactly that.

The question was, why had Jackson allowed himself to fall into such a trap—or worse, seemingly jumped into it?

Despite their misgivings and long odds, the group unanimously voted to start before dawn for *Cinco Picos Prisión* and, hopefully, some answers.

Chapter Fifteen

6:48 a.m.

BY THE TIME the sun rose over the barren Mexican wilderness, the five women were already almost two hours into their journey. They had left shortly after five, with Ashley insisting she was okay to drive. They had slept in shifts, and Hillary had gotten the least sleep of all, in part because she was doing more research and in part because, despite what she had projected for the last two days, she was growing more and more concerned about Jackson.

Their route took them north, almost to the U.S. border. They would follow roughly along the California border, then more closely along the Arizona border and through the massive *El Pinacate y Gran Desierto de Altar Biosphere Reserve* before heading southeast and south into the Sonoran Desert. The drive time was almost ten hours, and they would lose an hour passing into Mountain Time Zone. And there was a slight chance of encountering highway bandits. But Ashley said she wasn't slowing down for anything short of a tank, and the alternative was driving back into the U.S. and adding two hours to the drive time, plus a pair of border crossings.

They made their first stop in Mexicali to fill up on gas and use some disgusting restrooms. Then they drove east on Highway 2 through vast stretches of nothingness, seeing few cars on a desolate stretch of two-lane road. But, except for a pair of beat-up pickups parked on the shoulder, nothing even remotely hinting at bandits or a roadblock either. When they reached the small town of Caborca, some hundred miles south-southwest of Tucson, Arizona, they broke for a late lunch at a cantina selling street tacos. The temperature in the middle of the Sonoran Desert was close to 100 degrees, even in late October, and the breeze blew as much dust and sand through town as it did refreshment. In their travel they had circled around the northern end of the Gulf of California, and were far enough inland that neither it nor the Pacific provided any respite from the heat.

It was mid-afternoon, and they plodded on. Ashley remained at the wheel, with Maggie now spelling Hillary as navigator. Free from any responsibility and with nothing of interest to look at, Hillary reorganized her thoughts regarding *Cinco Picos* and Jackson. In addition to what she'd told the group earlier, she'd discovered more details about the prison's private ownership.

The Mexican government had contracted with *Guardián Uno*, a private security group based in Colombia. *Cinco Picos* was one of several prisons they ran in Central and South America, and running prisons was just one arm of their business. They also provided private security, for everyone from elected officials to drug lords, and maintained an aboveboard import/export and shipping business. The head of the corporation was a man named Andres Sepúlveda, a third-generation Colombian. Sepúlveda, however, had no direct affiliation with *Cinco Picos*. It was under the supervision of Carlos Villaverde, a Mexican-American with dual citizenship and familial ties to the U.S., Mexico, and several Latino nations. Villaverde's official title was Supervisor, which essentially made him the warden of *Cinco Picos*.

As for its contract with the government, it was pretty hands off. The Mexican government could send any prisoners they chose to the prison, and for any duration. They could also request a transfer of any inmate, but from what Hillary had found, had done so rarely. Everything else— security of the prison, treatment and privileges of the inmates, staffing, and so forth—was under the purview of *Guardián Uno*. There were some basic human rights standards that had to be observed, but Hillary guessed those could largely be ignored or excused and explained away if violated.

Speaking of privileges, visitation rights were solely at the discretion of *Guardián Uno* as well, or more accurately, at the discretion of Carlos

Villaverde. From what Hillary had been able to find, he seemed more than competent, well-trained, well-paid. He ran a good prison. Whether or not he was an upright person, someone who could be reasoned with, someone who could be pleaded with, remained to be seen. So did his availability on a Sunday afternoon.

"You look intent," Sam noted, and Hillary realized she had been staring straight ahead as she cataloged her thoughts.

"I'm thinking."

"What about?" Connie asked.

"Jackson."

"Really?" Maggie asked.

"In a roundabout way. Why, is that surprising?"

"Given your hostility toward him. I'm kind of surprised you voted to come this far."

"I've told you—I've told you all—that while Jackson and I don't get along and I disagree with him on many things, I don't hate him. He was almost my brother-in-law. I still consider him family."

"Or do you consider him something else?" Connie asked.

"Like what?"

"Oh, it's nothing."

"It was something," Hillary said.

Connie sighed. "It may not be my place, but I can't help but wonder if you're not staging some of this disdain for him."

"Staging?"

"You know, dear, how little schoolboys dip little schoolgirls' pigtails in inkwells."

"Pigtails in inkwells?" Maggie asked, her neck craned around the front seat.

"Trying to hide affections," Connie said. "Mask them with hatred."

"I said the same thing," Ashley said, briefly taking her eyes off the road to meet Connie's in the rearview mirror.

"You don't, do you?" Maggie asked, now looking straight at Hillary.

"Don't what?"

"Have a thing for Jackson?"

"No, I do not. I am engaged to be married."

"You wouldn't be the first person whose eyes wandered into another cowboy's pasture," Connie said.

"What does that even mean?"

"Yeah, I'm confused on the metaphors," Maggie said.

"You just seem to have a lot of hostility for claiming not to be that hostile," Ashley said.

"I have no romantic feelings for Jackson."

"Maybe you just aren't aware," Connie said.

"And maybe I am fully aware of my own feelings or lack thereof for someone. Now can we end this episode of *Saved by the Bell* and concentrate on what lies ahead of us? It's not like we can drive up to the front gate and demand to see him."

"We can't?" Connie asked.

"No," Hillary said, going over some of the facts she had researched and been ruminating on before her traveling companions' inner teenagers had come out. Even fleeting thoughts of being romantically involved with Jackson repulsed her, but she had long ago learned the more she denied and defended herself against wild accusations, the more guilty it made her appear. So she hoped a change of topic would have multiple benefits.

"So what do we do when we get there?" Sam asked.

"We can inquire at the main gate. They have a visitor check-in, but it sounds like getting to see an inmate is more luck and the whim of whoever's on duty than anything. Especially without an appointment."

"Do they have set aside visitors' hours?" Ashley asked.

"Yes, until five today, in fact. So that may work in our favor."

"If we make it," Ashley said, stepping on the gas.

They turned south in a little dump called Santa Ana, now on the four-lane Highway 15. Maggie announced it should be about half an hour as a low ridge of mountains began to rise against the sky on the eastern horizon. As they drove through mile after mile of scrub and sand, five distinct peaks became evident in the range. Several minutes later, a blue road sign indicated the turnout to *Cinco Picos Prisión.*

Ashley put on her turn signal and slowed. As she turned east on a two-lane road cutting through the desert, Hillary felt the knot that had been growing in her stomach all day—all weekend, in fact—tighten. They had reached the end of their journey. Nothing lay ahead on the dead-end road but Mexico's most secure prison, a place where criminals and dissidents went to be forgotten.

And Jackson was among them.

Chapter Sixteen

CINCO PICOS PRISIÓN was escape-proof.

Shaped like a giant, five-point star, it stood three stories tall, with concrete walls two-feet thick, reinforced by rebar. All cells were on the inside of the star, facing covered corridors that were constantly patrolled and monitored by closed-circuit cameras. In the center of the star was the command center, where armed guards could watch the camera feeds, electronically control gates and doors, and see into the points of the star, giving them a view of every cell door.

Inmates spent twenty-three hours a day in their cells, permitted only one hour out in the yard, a dirt-covered plot of ground with no real activities available—no basketball hoops, no sets of barbells or other exercise equipment, not so much as a soccer ball to kick around. They could look up past the featureless concrete and steel to see the blue sky, but that was as close to freedom as they would ever come.

There was only one way into the star and one way out, through a gate at the intersection of two points. It was actually two gates, made of solid steel, only one of which could be opened at a time. Both were heavily guarded. Short of somehow breaching both gates, the only other theoretical ways out were to vault over the walls, tunnel from the yard—under supervision of guards—or dig through two feet of concrete and squeeze between rebar spaced every foot.

Even should an inmate accomplish this, the star-shaped prison was surrounded by a pentagonal wall. It stood twelve feet tall, topped with barbed wire. At each point of the pentagon was a guard tower, manned by guards with automatic weapons. Any inmate who somehow escaped the interior of the prison would have guards from at least two towers firing at him as he raced across fifty yards of open terrain and tried to scale a twelve-foot wall. And even that wall was not the true exterior of the prison. It was itself encompassed in hundreds of yards of chain-link fence, intertwined and topped with barbed wire. And just in case a prisoner somehow managed to get past the wall or someone tried to breach from the outside, over one-thousand landmines had been buried in the desert. And desert surrounded *Cinco Picos Prisión* in every direction for at least twenty miles.

Escape-proof didn't begin to describe it.

One road led through the barbed wire fence and a steel-reinforced door in the pentagonal concrete wall, up to the entrance to the prison. Before it reached the barbed wire fence, however, it stopped at a small parking lot beside a simple, one-story "guardhouse." It served as both a processing center for incoming inmates and as a check-in center for visitors. Were they admitted to the prison to visit a prisoner, they would be taken by van to the prison gate, where they would be off-loaded and guided underground to a visitation room on the first floor of one of the prongs of the star.

The five women passed an actual guardhouse half a mile out from the prison. A man in generic desert-colored fatigues permitted them past the gate after they explained the reason for their purpose and submitted to a basic search of the underside of the Rogue. Ashley then drove to the parking lot, just shy of spike strips on the main road, and parked in a designated section of the lot. In addition to several "civilian" vehicles, two plain white vans, no windows, and four all-terrain Jeeps were parked at the other end of the lot.

The five women got out and stretched. The blacktop was fresh and blistering under the late afternoon sun. Ashley and Hillary took the lead, and Maggie cast her eyes around before bringing up the rear as the women walked toward a pair of double doors marked "*Visitantes.*" They were set on the far right of an L-shaped building, the left side of which was marked for incoming prisoners. Maggie stared at that doorway, wondering what Jackson's thoughts had been as he'd been brought into the building.

The interior was plain, white walls on all four sides. There was a gender-neutral restroom on the right, and a drinking fountain beside it. In the opposite wall, a doorway opened to what looked like a small storage room. Beside it, a closed door had no writing on it. Directly ahead was a wall with a window in the middle and another door beside it. The window resembled a ticket window at a sports venue, and a man dressed like the guard sat behind it. The room was empty, with a dozen airport-style seats against the walls. They were unadorned, except for several framed posters listing a variety of rules and regulations.

Ashley ignored them, walking up to the window. The man behind the counter, whose nametape identified him as Martinez, regarded the five women with confusion, but greeted them with a smile nonetheless. *"Buenos días, señoritas,"* he said through a vent in the window. *"¿Qué puedo hacer por ustedes?"*

After quickly establishing that Martinez spoke English, Ashley said, "We'd like to see an inmate. Jackson Douglas."

"I am sorry, but that is not possible at this time."

"Don't visiting hours go until five?" Ashley asked.

"Yes, but there is a process to it. We must verify documentation, search you, and arrange transportation for you and the prisoner. And that is assuming the request is granted."

"How do we make a request?" Connie asked.

"You can fill out a form here," Martinez said. "You can also call any time."

"I'm his attorney," Hillary said. "Can we expedite a request because of that?"

"What's your name?"

"Hillary McKenzie."

"M-A-C-K?"

"No A," she said.

Martinez typed her name into his computer. "Your name is not on the list, I'm sorry. You will have to fill out a request like everyone else."

Ashley leaned on the small counter on her side of the window. "Is it Officer Martinez?"

"Yes, ma'am."

"Officer Martinez, we drove from Ensenada today—almost ten hours. We're all due back in Los Angeles tomorrow morning, so we're already in country longer than we should be, and it's urgent we talk to Mr. Douglas. Is there any exception, is there anyone else we can talk to about this? Please."

The door to the left opened. "You can speak to me."

They turned to look at the man who had just stepped through the door. He was not dressed in fatigues but a suit, no tie. He was tall, well-built, with dark skin and faded black hair. His features and his accent were both Hispanic, but mildly so. He was handsome, and even before he introduced himself, Maggie knew who he was.

"I am Carlos Villaverde, the supervisor of *Cinco Picos Prisión*. Would you care to step into my office?"

"Thank you," Ashley said.

Villaverde held the door open for her, and she let Hillary go through while holding it for each of the others. They followed Villaverde down a hallway and through the second door on the right. He had walked behind a polished walnut desk in front of a large window looking out on the desert. There were seats for four in front of the desk, but he pushed his chair around to make room for each of them, then leaned back on his desk. The entire office seemed out of place in a prison. It was comfortable, cool, carpeted, decorated with photos of landmarks and scenery from around the world. One wall was reserved for a bank of monitors, most of which were currently dark.

Maggie's eye was drawn from surveying the office to Villaverde, who smiled as they all sat down. "I have to say, it is not often five beautiful women show up at our prison requesting to see an inmate. What is your interest in Mr. Douglas?"

"I'm his lawyer," Hillary said. She extended a business card to Villaverde, who studied it before placing it beside him on his desk.

"There is no representation listed on Mr. Douglas's record."

"That is because I was just recently made aware of his incarceration. I'm here now."

He peered down at the business card again. "This says you are from Los Angeles."

"Yes."

"Are these associates of yours, of . . . Conway, Davenport & Rankin?"

"No. This is Detective Ashley Larson, who was Mr. Douglas's liaison when he assisted the Los Angeles Police Department."

"Assisted?"

"Mr. Douglas is an accomplished private investigator." Hillary nodded at Maggie. "This is Anne "Maggie" Magstadt, a former columnist and investigative reporter with the *Los Angeles Times* and now a correspondent with Fox News. Connie DiMarco and Samantha MacRaney are also associates of Mr. Douglas and have worked with him on a number of cases."

Villaverde leaned back with a thin smile. "I am quite impressed. You have come to see about Mr. Douglas's release?"

"That is our ultimate goal, yes," Hillary said. "But we'd like to begin by simply seeing him."

"I'm afraid that is not possible."

"Why not?"

"Several reasons. As Officer Martinez told you, visiting hours end at five o'clock, and we simply couldn't make arrangements in time. We also are not in the habit of allowing visitors to see inmates without an appointment and a background check, even if those visitors do claim to represent the inmate. And third, the Mexican government has requested that Mr. Douglas not be allowed any visitors."

"I thought this prison was privately run," Ashley said.

"It is."

"Then isn't it up to you who gets to see visitors and who doesn't?"

"Technically, yes. But we seek to maintain a good relationship with the Mexican government, and thus make it a policy to honor their requests whenever possible."

"When you say the government requested, you mean Judge Benedicto Bautista, don't you?" Maggie said.

"I'm afraid those technicalities are above my pay grade," Villaverde said with a wince-like smile.

"*Señor* Villaverde," Hillary said, "I don't think you quite understand the firestorm we are capable of bringing down on this prison, on *Guardián Uno*, and on you personally. Maggie is the reporter who exposed Leonardo Vasquez and *Mexól* last year. Detective Larson has many connections not only in Los Angeles, but in state and federal government. And I," she said, leaning forward, "would also direct you to the sterling reputation and record of Conway, Davenport & Rankin. Our specialty is criminal defense, but we also have a civil litigation division that has crushed a number of illegitimate and crooked enterprises across the United States and around the world."

She paused to lick her lips, then continued in a voice both velvety smooth and razor sharp. "Now tell me, *Señor* Villaverde, are you really so adamant about bowing to the whims and desires of a corrupt state judge that you are willing to risk the sort of exposure I'm talking about?"

Villaverde stood and paced around his desk, looking out his massive bank of windows at the late afternoon sun's reflection on the desert floor. Slowly, he turned around. "Miss McKenzie—It is miss, correct?"

"Yes," she said coolly.

"I appreciate your passion and I no doubt believe that you believe you can do all you have claimed. But you forget that you are in the sovereign nation of Mexico. You have no jurisdiction here," he said, eyeing Ashley and then Hillary. "You can threaten legal action if you want, but I assure you, we have ample legal protection on our side. Might you win?" He shrugged. "Perhaps. But the threat of a lawsuit is not going to persuade me from doing my duties. Nor is the threat of an exposé in a national newspaper or running on a major American cable news network."

He leaned on his desk. "My advice to you is go home. Mexico—particularly the Sonoran Desert—is no place for a group of beautiful young women."

"Is that a threat?" Ashley asked.

"No, of course not," he said with a smile. "I bear you no ill will. But there are many in this country who are not as benevolent as I am." He came back around to sit/lean on the edge of his desk. "Now, you may take legal action, you may write a report, you may try to speak to Judge Bautista or the Supreme Court or whomever you choose. That is your right. But I will remind you that the Mexican legal system is not like your American system. If Judge Bautista—or any other judge or court—does not wish a prisoner to be free, there is nothing I can do, and nothing you can do. In the eleven years this prison has been operational, a total of two men have had their convictions reversed or their sentences commuted. There is good reason people refer to those at *Cinco Picos* as *los olvidados*."

Beside Maggie, Hillary was silently fuming. Maggie was at a low boil too, but listening carefully.

"I can tell you this," Villaverde said, "Mr. Douglas is alive. He is in good health, all things considered. But you are not permitted to see him, nor will you be. Go home, go on with your lives, and forget that Mr. Douglas ever lived. Because, for all intents and purposes, he no longer does."

The group was silent for a moment. Sam broke it. "Can we write him a message?"

"Yes, of course."

"Is he allowed to write us back?"

"Prisoners are permitted occasional writing supplies and can send letters, yes."

"Could we borrow a piece of paper and pen or pencil?" Sam asked. "We'll be brief."

"Of course," Villaverde said, and retrieved a standard sheet of eight-and-a-half by eleven paper and a pen. While the others looked on, Sam quickly drafted a message, telling Jackson that they had come to see him, they knew he had been railroaded by Judge Bautista, and that they were ready and willing to help. She concluded by pleading with him to write back and stating that they loved him. Each of the five women signed it, and Sam handed it back to Villaverde.

Without reading it, he folded it in thirds. "I will see that he gets this right away, you have my word."

"Thank you," Sam said.

"And I am sorry that I cannot accommodate your request. But I have rules that I must follow. And I do not suggest you go home or forget Mr. Douglas as a threat, but with your best interests in mind. Believe me, there is nothing you can do to free Mr. Douglas, and nothing will come of further efforts but heartache and grief."

"We will see about that," Hillary said.

Villaverde only nodded, then guided the women back out of his office, down the hallway, and to the waiting room.

"Is that it?" Connie asked when he'd closed the door.

"That's it," Hillary said, turning for the exit.

Maggie again brought up the rear. Stepping through the double doors, she squinted against the unrelenting sun as it beat down on the empty, barren desert. The heat was oppressive, and Maggie wanted to retch at the thought of Jackson spending one more day—let alone years or a lifetime—in *Cinco Picos Prisión*.

Chapter Seventeen

5:43 p.m.

THE WOMEN STOPPED on the outskirts of Santa Ana to top off the fuel tank and grab food for the road. They had driven from the prison mostly in silence, except with a brief discussion about which route to take. The quickest way back to Los Angeles was back the way they had come, to Mexicali, and then north into California. They opted instead to head straight north through Nogales and into Arizona, then through Tucson and Phoenix. It would add about an hour to their drive time, but would get them out of Mexico quicker, and thus be safer.

There had been no dissenting vote about going home. Hillary had laid out their options: challenge Bautista in Mexico, expose his corruption, pursue other legal activity, try to get the U.S. government involved—none of which could be pursued immediately and none of which would be advanced by them spending any more time in Mexico now. Not to mention, they all had lives and jobs and—in two cases—fiancés to return to.

She had not said it, but there was one final option—the one Carlos Villaverde had suggested: give up. Ashley couldn't foresee much success with any of Hillary's options, but she couldn't bring herself to give up on Jackson either.

She and Maggie were the last two to use the restrooms at the gas station convenience store, and they exited to see Sam and Hillary arguing, backlit by the setting sun.

"We cannot just leave him to rot there," Sam said.

"What other option do we have?" Hillary asked. "Everything I told Villaverde was bluster, and he didn't fall for it. He's right. We have no legal grounds. It would take months if not years for me to even get licensed, and then we'd still have little to no chance of winning in a corrupt system with corrupt judges who have even more power than American judges."

"What about taking legal action, like your firm has done before?"

"Bluster. Trust me, we wouldn't stand a chance."

"We cannot give up," Sam said, on the verge of tears.

"We have no choice, and let's not forget, Jackson did nothing to keep this from happening. In fact, he seemed to bring it on himself."

Sam turned away and found a consoling shoulder in Connie. Hillary shook her head and rolled her eyes, the last rays of the sunlight shining through perfectly blond hair.

"She's right," Maggie said. "We can't give up."

Hillary sighed. "Then what should we do?"

"I don't know. I can pitch a fit on social media, get a 'Free Jackson' hashtag going, try to get the major talking heads involved, doing live remotes from down here."

"If Jackson had cachet or was a celebrity of some sort, maybe. But he's just another guy, and don't forget, the events that led him to *Cinco Picos* aren't exactly tragic. They're his own doing."

Maggie sighed.

"We can talk to Reggie," Sam said, sniffing away tears.

"He already gave up on him, from what you say."

"He doesn't know all the facts."

"Talk to him if you want. But everything we've found indicated Jackson ran his life into the ground, ignoring advice from his best friend, avoiding all of you. Maybe Villaverde was right. Maybe the best thing for all of us to do is forget we ever knew Jackson."

Sam let out a sob, and Connie hugged her again. Maggie turned away, toward the Rogue, but not before Ashley caught a tear reflected in the sunlight as it rolled down her cheek. She felt her own eyes getting wet, but steeled herself against tears. "We should get moving," she said.

Slowly, the other four women loaded into the vehicle.

Ashley was last, taking one final look toward the symbolic setting sun. She shared Sam and Maggie's sentiments that they couldn't give up. But she also recognized the truth of what Hillary had said. In two weeks, Ashley would be married, then on her honeymoon, then back to work as a detective in Redding—far away from L.A. and reminders of Jackson. As much as she hated to admit it, Hillary was probably right that there was nothing more they could do—nothing that would ultimately work. And she hated to admit it even more, but she—and the rest of them—would probably slowly forget about Jackson. After all, he was now part of *los olvidados*.

As she rounded the front of the vehicle, she couldn't stop the tears.

*   *   *

6:24 p.m.

A DOZEN miles south of the road to *Cinco Picos* on Highway 15 was a seedy bar and restaurant named *El Hombre Solitario*. Carlos Villaverde parked under a crooked light pole on the gravel lot and walked toward the sound of *Norteño* music and the smell of grilled food. He entered a darkly lit room, ignoring the music and the soccer match on a TV above the bar and truckers, passing motorists, and professional girls who frequented *El Hombre Solitario*. He instead walked down a side hallway, toward the bathrooms, and stopped in an alcove where the music and smoke were only half as strong. He lifted a pay phone off its cradle, plugged several coins into it, and dialed a number on a slip of paper in his pocket.

Six rings passed, then a click signaled someone on the other end had answered. But there was only silence.

"Hace mucho calor en el desierto de Sonora," Villaverde said at last.

Several seconds passed. "How hot, exactly?" a muffled, perhaps disguised, voice said in English.

"Cincuenta grados."

"Tell me about it," the voice said.

"Five American women arrived late this afternoon," Villaverde continued in English. "They asked to see Jackson Douglas."

As always, there was a short pause before the answer. "What did you tell them?"

"That Mr. Douglas was not permitted any visitors and that they should go home and forget about him."

"How did they respond?"

"They left a message, on paper."

"Do you have it?"

"Yes. Would you like me to read it?"

"Yes."

Villaverde fished the sheet of paper from his pocket, unfolded it, and in the alcove at the end of the smoky hallway at *El Hombre Solitario*, read it verbatim, in English, including the names affixed at the bottom.

A dozen seconds passed when he was finished.

"Destroy it," the voice said.

"Consider it done."

"Did they say anything else?"

"No. They left, and have not come back. That is as much as I know."

"Very good. Thank you for reporting so quickly."

"Of course."

"I'll have an additional ten thousand dollars wired to your account in a few days, as a bonus."

"I appreciate that very much."

"You'll call this number again if they or anyone else asks about Mr. Douglas?"

"I will."

"Gracias, Señor Villaverde."

The line clicked, and Villaverde hung up a dead phone.

www.ingramcontent.com/pod-product-compliance
Lightning Source LLC
Chambersburg PA
CBHW051838170626
46807CB00003B/1242